Substitute Sweetheart

Sweetheart Series · Book Two

Shannon Sue Dunlap

Published by Scrivenings Press LLC
15 Lucky Lane
Morrilton, Arkansas 72110
https://ScriveningsPress.com

Printed in the United States of America

Paperback ISBN 978-1-64917-422-2

eBook ISBN 978-1-64917-423-9

Editors: Regina Merrick and Heidi Glick

Cover design by Shannon Sue Dunlap and Linda Fulkerson - www.bookmarketinggraphics.com

To my fellow teachers at Beta Academy,
your hard work, creativity, and never-ending love for your students
has changed lives

Chapter One

How could she survive the wedding without an interpreter?

"Y'all" and "Bless her heart" floated past her ears as Victoria Park walked through the reception and sat at the head table. She observed the festivities with the amused interest of a tourist in a strange land. The number of cowboy hats being worn indoors highlighted how far out of civilized society she'd traveled.

Her lightning-paced life in New York City felt a world away. Two days in the small burg of Sweetheart, Texas, had almost killed her. She was dying for a decent cup of espresso. But her exile crept ever closer to the end. One more night, then she'd climb in her rental car without a backward glance.

Victoria tugged at the poofy chiffon monstrosity she'd been forced to wear as the maid of honor. It was a cranberry-red, vintage swing dress with scratchy crinoline and a matching pillbox hat. She hated the outfit, and she didn't feel much better about her new sister-in-law. Why had her clever brother fallen for such a pushy, opinionated woman?

Victoria's father liked their new family member. For the life of her, she couldn't understand why. He mingled among the wedding-goers with the comfort of a man who'd pastored a church for thirty-five years. If only she'd inherited his social skills.

"Hey, Vic!"

One of her fellow bridesmaids slid beside her. What was the woman's name? Anna something?

"Hello, Anna," Victoria said.

"De-anna." The cheery blonde smiled. "But close enough. Let's take a picture together while we're gussied up. I haven't looked this good in years."

Really? What was her normal fashion choice? Blueberry-colored burlap?

Deanna held her phone at arm's length, tilted her head, and snapped a picture. "Thanks. I hope you—" She shrank back until her body was half hidden behind Victoria's. "Uh-oh! There's Mrs. Biddle. She's the biggest gossip in town. I bet you twenty dollars she's headed over to ask me when it will be my turn to wear white. Take care."

She dashed away mere seconds before a short, middle-aged woman with hair dyed burgundy red chugged up to the table. The lady gasped from the exertion. Her purple sequined dress shimmered under the party lights.

"Oh, Deanna. Wait!" Mrs. Biddle slapped a hand on her sparkly hip. "She must not have heard me. I wanted to ask when I'll be getting a wedding invitation with her name on it. Only the good Lord knows who the other name will be. That girl jumps from man to man like a frog on a lily pad."

Victoria's lips twitched. Deanna had this woman's number. Good thing she'd bolted for safety.

Mrs. Biddle turned her full attention on Victoria. "You're the groom's sister, right? A college professor from the Big Apple? Single with no current prospects?"

The gossip hotline was alive and well in Sweetheart. How had this busybody found out so much? Her brother never shared personal information about his family. Could it have been her new sister-in-law?

Mrs. Biddle leaned in. "You and Andrew Zimmerman made quite an attractive pair walking down the aisle together. Any hope there?"

Victoria blinked, unsure how to answer the stranger invading both her space and her private life with all the subtlety of a steamroller.

The woman's burgundy-topped head whipped to the left. "There's Deanna. Excuse me, please."

She bustled away, and Victoria released a breath. New York possessed its fair share of nosy people, but they usually cloaked their inquiries in a little more buildup.

Speaking of New York, how were things going at home?

She slipped her phone from the hidden pocket of her dress. No texts. Strange.

The board meeting was scheduled for this afternoon. Surely the university had made their final decision by now. Her contract was up for renewal. This time, she expected a much bigger offer than another teaching stint.

Applause broke out, and she laid the phone on the table. Her brother, Ryan, walked through the door, arm in arm with his new wife, Katherine. Victoria's sister-in-law had become mayor at the notable young age of thirty. As a career woman, Victoria respected her drive. But in a town of five thousand people, how hard could it be to get elected?

Ryan led his bride onto the hardwood floor. An eighties girl-group anthem played, and Victoria squinted at the music. Hardly a romantic first dance. Maybe it's how they did things in the sticks.

If she ever married, she'd choose a string quartet playing a refined mix of Chopin and Beethoven. But there wasn't much chance of that happening. Romance wasn't on her agenda. She'd chosen a career path and never looked back.

Her outdated hat with the cranberry netting started to droop. She yanked the offensive accessory into place. Why did her sister-in-law pick such a ridiculous outfit?

"Feeling weepy yet?" a rich baritone voice whispered in her ear.

Hints of a subtle, woodsy cologne tickled Victoria's nose. The best man, Andrew Zimmerman, settled on the chair beside her. His tall, muscular frame fit the Texas cowboy stereotype to a tee, and honey-brown hair flopped over his forehead in a relaxed style that contradicted his fancy tuxedo.

A genuine smile stretched across her face. "I never cry. I'm not the sentimental type."

The handsome elementary music teacher had played her partner in crime throughout the rehearsal, whispering explanations for the local customs, and making her laugh with funny anecdotes. Yet, in all those stories, he'd kept his words positive and kind.

He slumped and stretched his long legs out with a sigh. "Ready to burn the bridesmaid dress?"

"Show me the nearest bonfire," she murmured.

"You'll have to get in line." He loosened the bow tie around his neck. "I want to be rid of this formal straightjacket." He slipped the tie in a pocket and released the collar button of his starchy, white dress shirt.

Victoria glanced at her phone again.

Still nothing.

Andrew nudged her. "Planning your escape route?"

She tucked the phone away. "Not exactly. The board at the university where I work had their monthly meeting today. I've been a professor for ten years, and they're considering me for a promotion. Associate dean."

His eyebrows rose. "Impressive. If the dean at my college had been half as beautiful as you, I might've skipped fewer lectures."

"I bet you were the class clown." She poked him with her elbow even as the tips of her ears heated.

Flirting wasn't part of her normal repertoire, but she was on vacation. Andrew had proved himself a witty, well-informed companion, and there was no harm enjoying her last few hours in Sweetheart bantering with the good-looking charmer.

Victoria removed the annoying hat and tossed it on the table. She smoothed a strand of hair into place. How did one go about attracting the opposite sex? It had been forever since she'd tried. Perhaps complimenting his job?

A rock-and-roll electric guitar played through the sound system. The riff swelled into an earsplitting crescendo.

Victoria pointed at the speakers. "The music isn't really to my taste. What's your opinion as a professional?"

Andrew grinned. "I don't use a lot of eighties rock with kindergartners. Pretty sure Katherine chose the song. She has a whole collection of empowered girl band T-shirts."

"Why doesn't that surprise me?" She took a sip from her water glass and checked her phone one more time.

How late had the meeting run? Her friend on the board assured her she was a shoo-in for associate dean. The only thing left was the official vote. Then she could move into her new corner office and get to work on her real goal.

Dean.

The long hours she'd put in to get this far would seem mere child's play compared to what she'd have to sacrifice for the ultimate position. Who knew? This might be the last opportunity she ever had to dance with a handsome man while she was young enough to enjoy it.

Forget her pride. She'd never see these people again. Why not make the most of the evening?

Victoria cleared her throat. "Despite the inappropriate song choice, I might consider dusting off my old moves." She gave an over-exaggerated batting of her lashes and faked a thick Southern drawl. "If the right gentleman asked me to dance."

Andrew hopped up and bent at the waist, extending a hand. His brown eyes warmed her like an extra-large cup of café mocha. "Say no more, fair lady. Would you do me the honor of electric sliding with me?"

She placed her fingers in his and stood. "Lead the way."

Andrew's legs cranked out a heroic Running Man, but he couldn't compare to the groom's sister, Victoria Park. Her uninhibited abandon was a delightful surprise. She'd been a bit on the standoffish side when they were first introduced. Not unfriendly. *Buttoned-up* might be a better description.

Tonight, the sleek New Yorker shocked him with her endless supply of energy and antiquated dance routines. No matter how ridiculous the song, she found an appropriate move to match without hesitation or embarrassment. The captivating woman sparkled with confidence in her puffy red dress.

Victoria held her arms Egyptian style and poked them in either direction. Her shiny black hair swished. "I hope no one is recording this. It would make great blackmail material."

"You've got nothing to be ashamed of." Andrew copied her pose. "I haven't had this much fun at a wedding since ... ever."

She laughed and jutted her chin to the beat. "Ditto."

"Mr. Z!" His five-year-old student Sophie ran up in the same floral dress she wore to church every Sunday. After a recent growth spurt, the hem barely brushed the top of her skinny knees. Her tight, wiry curls bounced as she took hold of his tuxedo trousers. "I looked all over for you. Dance with me!"

He glanced at Victoria and back to the youngster. "Sorry, Sophie. I already have a partner."

"Oh." Her small mouth drooped.

Victoria observed the little girl's bereft expression and raised a hand. "Hold it. This young lady searched for you." She took a step away and extended both arms with a bow. "I don't mind sharing."

Sophie giggled.

Andrew squatted down to meet the child eye-to-eye. "I've got something important to finish with this lovely lady. Can I come find you in a few minutes?"

"Promise?" She poked out a pinky.

He kissed his thumb and hooked his pinky with her tiny one. "Promise. See? I sealed it with a kiss."

An appeased Sophie took off, wound around the dancers' legs, and disappeared into the crowd.

"Who was that?" Victoria asked.

"One of my students." He puffed out his chest. "I'm her favorite teacher."

"You should protect your preferred status instead of making her wait. What was so important?"

The music changed to a dreamy ballad. Andrew pointed at the ceiling. "A slow dance." He placed his hand behind her back. "With you."

She moved naturally into his arms, and he settled her close. The top of her silky, black hair tickled his chin. Her soft frame pressed against his, and he found himself wishing Victoria's stay in Sweetheart wasn't temporary.

Might as well wish for the moon. This sophisticated woman belonged in the big city, as her habitual checking of her cell phone reminded him. But he could enjoy her company for a few more hours.

An older man in a suit and bolo tie danced by with his wife. "You got a mighty pretty partner there, Andrew."

"Thanks, Mayor." Andrew saluted.

Victoria's gaze followed the couple as they moved away. "I thought my new sister-in-law was the mayor."

"She is." He danced in a lazy circle. "That man held the office before Katherine, and folks were used to calling him Mayor Johnson. It's kind of an honorary title, like they give former presidents."

"I see." Victoria relaxed. "If that's the case, I have a grudge to settle with him."

"How do you figure?"

"Wasn't he the one who hired my brother to come to Sweetheart? If he'd never offered him the job, Ryan wouldn't have met Katherine. I'm trying to comprehend what they found in common."

"I guess love doesn't have to make sense. Sometimes it just happens."

She blew a skeptical puff of air from her lips. "Oh, please. Don't tell me you believe the movie propaganda. Real life doesn't come with a soundtrack. Love is a choice."

Her statement intrigued him. It echoed his own prosaic beliefs on the subject. A kind of everyday, unromantic idea of love that didn't fit well with weddings and fairy tales.

"Interesting. Tell me more."

"My brother didn't take one glance at Katherine and forget his job, his family, and his life in New York. He chose to be with her, to give up everything for a chance at happiness. For all our sakes, I hope it works out. I'd hate to have dressed as a fifties baby doll for nothing."

Andrew chuckled. "You'd look good in anything. Even a feed sack."

She shook her head. "I feel like a reject from one of those old Hollywood musicals."

"Would this be time for the big dance number? Glad to oblige."

He lifted his arm and spun her in a circle and out the open double doors onto the porch. String lights stretched in rows over their heads. She followed his lead, mirroring his steps in a perfect, graceful rhythm.

Andrew paused mid-twirl, one hand at her waist and the other holding her delicate fingers. Her soft palm molded to his—a perfect fit.

He cleared his throat. "I think it's fair to warn you the ambiance is getting to me."

She answered with a low, melodic laugh. "How do you mean?"

"In this light, you're so beautiful, I want to forget we're almost strangers."

Her eyelashes fluttered. Not in a provocative style. More like a burst of surprise. But she didn't pull away. It took her a second to respond. "And if we weren't strangers?"

He drew a deep, steadying breath and leaned down. His lips touched hers, gentle but firm. Her mouth softened without hesitation. The encouragement wrecked any polite pretense, and he pressed her closer. Victoria's arms wrapped around his neck in a welcoming embrace.

Something buzzed against Andrew's side, interrupting the perfect moment. He shifted back a bit. "Unless you've got restless leg syndrome, your phone is vibrating."

"Hmm?" Her eyes refocused. She jerked away and slipped the cell from a hidden pocket in her voluminous dress.

She swiped at the screen, and her face brightened. "It's here. Finally!" Victoria tapped on the phone and read the text. The smile faded. Her hand dropped to her side.

"What's wrong?" He noted a slight sway in her body and took her by the elbow. "Are you okay?"

"I'm—" She looked up, pupils dilated. "I'm fired."

Chapter Two

Yes. She hated her new sister-in-law. It was certain now.

Victoria sat on the charcoal-gray couch of her brother's living room as Katherine Bruno Park paced in front of her. A pair of energetic Yorkshire terriers followed her through the room, making wide laps around the train of her wedding dress.

"It's Providence!" The white satin swooshed as Katherine waved her arms. "The doctor put Mattie Kilgallen, our elementary principal, on bed rest for the last trimester of her pregnancy. Totally unexpected. And no one wants to take her position for the second semester of school. Too much work for too little pay."

Victoria spoke slowly as if to a child. "So why try to make me do it?"

"You got fired." Katherine's tone was matter of fact. "You need a job."

"I need a job in New York." Victoria flipped her hand palm up. "Where I live."

"Consider this an extended vacation." Katherine stopped pacing. "I imagine January in New York is way colder than here. It will do your lungs good to get out of the polluted city and breathe fresh air. You might even find you prefer Sweetheart. Your brother did."

Love had turned his brain to mush. But Victoria had no such inducement.

Perhaps logic would work with her overenthusiastic relative-by-marriage. "I assume there's some sort of license or certification the state of Texas requires to be a principal. I don't qualify."

Katherine batted the argument away like a tennis ball. "We'll give you an almost-principal title."

Ryan, wearing jeans and a light sweater, appeared from the bedroom. He wheeled a hard-shell suitcase into the room and kissed his bride on the cheek. "You mean *interim principal?*"

"Right." Katherine nodded. "That sounds more official. Interim principal. For all intents and purposes, Mattie will still be the official principal while she stays home in bed, but you'll be at the school running things. If anyone asks why we chose you, we say you've taught at a New York university for the past ten years. You're more than qualified to run a small-town elementary school."

Victoria rubbed the spot between her eyebrows. "There's a world of difference between a college campus and a kindergarten."

"It's not just kindergarten. The school goes up to second grade."

"Why is the mayor recruiting me?" Victoria shifted on the couch, and the netting of her crinoline scratched her legs. She yanked at the abrasive material. "Doesn't the school board handle this kind of thing?"

Her brother chuckled. "Trust me. Katherine stuck her nose in everybody's business even before she was elected mayor."

His wife swatted at him. "If Sweetheart has a problem, it's my job as a good citizen to help find a solution."

Victoria crossed her arms. "I have a life in New York. An apartment. Not to mention an office at the university I'm supposed to clean out by Monday."

Katherine plopped on the cushion beside her. "So fly home, pack enough clothes for a few months, and make quick work of cleaning out your office. After what they did to you, they can hardly expect you to mop the floors. Right?"

Victoria couldn't argue. Ten long years of early morning classes, late-night tutoring, filling in for sick coworkers, and every thankless task no one else wanted. Her goal had been to gain the associate dean position by the time she turned forty. Now, with only two days until the second semester commenced, she'd be lucky to find a community college job.

Her brother sat on her other side and took her hand. "Look, Vic. I realize it isn't the ideal circumstance. But this could be good for you. You've been working too hard. Those lines near your mouth are starting to get deeper."

She snatched her hand away and patted her cheeks. "Thanks loads."

Ryan poked her. "I understand your reluctance. The rural society is unfamiliar territory. It will take you a few weeks to overcome the culture shock."

"Hey"—his wife leaned in their direction—"we speak English in Sweetheart. This isn't a foreign country."

He shushed her and jerked his head at Victoria.

Katherine stood with a huff. "I've got to change. Can't wear my wedding dress on the plane."

His gaze followed her with fond amusement as she left the

room. Victoria watched her once cynical brother react like a teenager in the throes of his first crush. She didn't understand Ryan's affection for the temperamental woman, but she envied the happiness he'd found. Was it just Katherine? Or was it this place?

Sweetheart.

Should she give the town a chance as he had done?

"Yes." Ryan nodded. "I think Sweetheart is worth the gamble."

He'd always been able to read her mind. She twisted her lips at him, refusing to answer.

He counted on his fingers. "Fact one, you are unemployed. Fact two, the school needs a principal. Fact three, you'd be helping out your darling baby brother."

She raised an eyebrow. "How does my moving to Podunk help you?"

"If you agree to be the interim principal, Katherine will calm down and focus on the honeymoon. If you don't, my bride will spend at least half the trip brainstorming who she can get to fill the position. Even if she's not saying it out loud, her mind is always whirring."

"And you signed up for a lifetime of that."

"It was my pleasure." He threw an arm around her shoulders. "Because when she points all that passion at me, it makes everything worth it. I hope you get the chance to experience the same joy someday."

She shook him off and stood. "No thanks. Love isn't in my five-year plan."

"Neither was being fired," Ryan said, "but here you are." He took her by both hands. "Life throws a lot of surprises at us, both good and bad. It's nicer when you have someone by your side to walk with you through the rough spots. Come on, Vic." He swung her arms back and forth. "Do it for me."

Victoria gritted her teeth. Her darling baby brother played dirty. She'd never been able to deny him anything.

She pulled her hands from his, covered her face, and groaned. "Does this mean I have to wear a cowboy hat?"

Chapter Three

Andrew grabbed a cup of coffee from the snack table. The lanyard with his ID slapped his chest as he picked a seat at the end of a row. Staff meetings—filled with boring details about standardized tests, online trainings, and attendance reminders—rarely had anything to do with him.

Music teachers experienced the best of both worlds by interacting with energetic, malleable young minds but avoiding the monotonous, administrative details a grade-level teacher performed.

"An emergency staff meeting?" Belinda Carlyle, the art teacher, sat beside him. "What is it this time? More pencils shoved in the boys' bathroom toilets?"

He chuckled. "Maybe they've discovered another rat snake near the playground."

"Hold on, everybody!" Ronnie Ford, the school secretary, fiddled with a computer at the front of the room and hooked a cable to the TV. "Let me get the internet feed working."

She signed in to an online meeting app, and Mattie Kilgallen's face filled the screen. Her curly brown hair frizzed out on each side. Behind her was a headboard, a pile of pink, lacy pillows at her back.

"Hello, my dear friends." Her familiar sunny voice rang out, and the teachers quieted. "I hope you're enjoying the teacher workday before the kids come back. I wish I could be there in person, but it's impossible. You might notice my unusual location. The doctor's ordered me to stay in bed until the baby arrives."

Voices buzzed.

Mattie held a finger to her lips. "Shhhhhhh. I don't have to be there to imagine how noisy it is. Don't worry about me. If I follow the doctor's instructions, the baby and I will be fine. But just like when a teacher takes a day off, I needed a substitute. And the mayor found a remarkable person." She waited an overlong minute with a mischievous grin. "Her new sister-in-law, Victoria Park."

The buzz started again.

Andrew's eyes widened, and he scanned the room. No sign of the beautiful woman he'd kissed at the wedding. Was this some kind of prank?

The video image of their principal plumped the pillow behind her. "I'll be forever grateful she agreed to pinch hit for me. Ms. Park is unable to attend the staff meeting, because she's flying back from New York. She'll be on campus later today, and I want you to give her a warm Sweetheart welcome."

Andrew zoned out for the rest of the video call. The meeting ended, and teachers clumped in tiny, chattering groups. He wandered out to the playground for a little peace and settled on a swing. It creaked beneath his weight as he kept his gaze trained on the parking lot.

Waiting.

His brain zipped through the details Mattie had given

them. Delectable Victoria Park was the new interim principal. He shook his head, processing the news. After the wedding, a strange sense of melancholy had overwhelmed him. Almost bitterness. Why had God brought such an amazing woman into his life for a short two days?

Pumping a fist at the sky, he laughed. "I said I wanted more time with her, but I didn't know You were listening."

The woman who'd made his heart beat at molto presto was moving to Sweetheart. They'd be interacting every day in the school halls. Was this the modern-day equivalent of a miracle?

A beat-up gray sedan with a dented door drove into the lot. Andrew recognized the car and stood. The honeymooning Mayor Park must have loaned it to her sister-in-law. He loped across the playground as Victoria climbed from the car with a large cardboard box. She wore a black pinstripe suit with shiny, patent leather high heels. Her silky hair was styled in a bun at the nape of her neck. What a shame. He preferred how it looked, framing her soft cheeks.

He reached her side and held out his arms. "Victoria! Welcome."

She squinted as if trying to place him.

He took the box from her. "You didn't wear your bridesmaid's dress. I thought you were so fond of it."

Her eyes grew round.

"I work here." He motioned to the school building. "Remember I told you at the wedding I taught music?"

From her blank expression, she'd forgotten. Obviously, his presence hadn't been an inducement to take the job. A small blow to his ego, but the joy of seeing her helped him recover.

He smiled. "Let me show you to your office."

They walked together from the parking lot. Andrew pointed out various school aspects to familiarize her with the campus. When they entered the main double doors, curious heads poked out of classrooms as they passed.

"Don't worry," Andrew called down the hallway. "I'll introduce her at lunch."

He stopped beside the door marked Principal. "Here it is. They announced a special potluck at noon when you can meet the staff. That gives you an hour to get settled. Have I covered everything?"

She took the box from his arms and nodded.

"Great." He studied Victoria's still-shocked face. Was she feeling shy? "Don't be nervous. Everyone's anxious to meet you."

Andrew patted her elbow and walked away. It might take her a while to get her bearings. The poor thing hadn't said a word on the way in. She must be terrified.

VICTORIA DUMPED HER THINGS ON A WELL-USED, FLORAL COUCH BY the lone office window and flopped onto the swivel chair behind the desk. She collapsed on the top, burying her head in her arms. The gorgeous groomsman she'd allowed herself to cut loose with at the wedding was now her subordinate. Look where her uncharacteristic lapse in judgement had led. To complete and total mortification.

Why had she kissed him?

Her behavior was unprofessional, unacceptable, and humiliating.

Could she regain his respect after he'd seen her do the Macarena? And not just him. Had any other teachers witnessed her uninhibited exhibition at the reception?

In a small town, the probability was high.

She bonked her head against the desk and moaned. "Why? Why? Why?"

She had lost the associate dean position at the university, but she refused to lose her dignity. Victoria would show Sweetheart Elementary what she was made of and how hard she could work.

She sat up and grabbed a pen and paper. First things first, present the teachers with a polished first impression. Second, have the custodian give her a full tour of the building and make note of any necessary repairs. Third, study the lunch menus to—

Her itemized list reached twenty before she found a stopping point. Perhaps it would be better to concentrate on the teachers today. They were the most pertinent cog in the machinery.

She straightened her shoulders, stood, and tugged the hem of her pinstripe suit coat. If she wanted to erase any memory in her coworkers' minds of a poofy-dress-wearing principal doing the Cabbage Patch, she must present the complete opposite image.

Stalking from the office, Victoria entered the hallway and marched to the first classroom. She knocked on the door and entered. A short man in jeans and a sweatshirt sat with feet propped on the desk, a half-eaten granola bar in his hand.

Victoria allowed her gaze to travel the length of his relaxed torso. She gave a tight smile. Time to show the staff she wasn't a flighty airhead.

"Good afternoon. I'm Victoria Park, the interim principal. I hope jeans are only allowed on staff workdays. If not, we'll need to adjust the dress code."

The teacher lowered his feet. He stood at attention. With a twitchy hand, he brushed at the granola crumbs on his collar.

Excellent.

She could sense the respect already.

Chapter Four

Andrew whistled on his way to the cafeteria. Barely an hour since he'd seen Victoria, but he missed her already. It took every bit of willpower not to wander by her office and offer his help.

He stopped at the metal lunchroom doors. In the distance, he spotted the secretary, Ronnie Ford. The woman crouched as much as her five-foot-nine frame would allow, her salt-and-pepper head bent as she slunk off.

"Ronnie!" he called. "Aren't you heading the wrong way?"

She bolted upright and jerked his direction.

Andrew beckoned. "It's time for lunch. I hope Betty baked her famous apple turnovers."

Ronnie tiptoed to his side and whispered, "I don't care if she did. I'm not eating lunch with that harpy for all the turnovers in Texas."

"What harpy?" His voice rose.

"Shhhhhhh!" She flapped her hands. "Victoria Park. She's been all over the school, throwing her weight around. I never met a bossier woman in my life. There'll be frost on the trees in July before I eat a meal with her."

She crept away, and Andrew watched in confusion. When he'd first met Victoria, she'd been a bit reserved but not unkind. How had his dance partner gotten on Ronnie's bad side? It must be a misunderstanding.

He'd give Victoria a heads-up. The gateway to goodwill at Sweetheart Elementary was Ronnie Ford. If she approved of you, her good opinion bought a golden ticket to smooth public relations with the staff and parents alike.

Andrew swung open the door and entered the quiet cafeteria—a far cry from the jovial chitchat of a normal staff luncheon. Teachers congregated in small groups around the edges of the room. They hunched over their plates in silence. At a long lunch table in the center sat Victoria.

Alone. Slim shoulders straight. Her body tight.

Oh, this was bad. Something must have gone desperately wrong.

Andrew walked to her side and straddled the bench connected to the table. "Hey, Victoria. How's your first day going?"

She looked at him, a prim pair of cat eye reading glasses perched on her nose. "Good afternoon, Mr. Zimmerman. If you wouldn't mind, please call me Ms. Park. I prefer to keep things professional."

A snort sounded from the corner. Andrew's gaze cut to the right and noted the coach whispering to the art teacher. They wore twin expressions of disgust.

Andrew lowered his voice. "I'm not sure what you're thinking, but I'm giving you a friendly warning. The staff responds better to a softer approach. Sweetheart is a close-knit community, and word spreads fast."

"Thank you for the advice." She turned away. "I'm not afraid of the small-town gossip mill."

Andrew cocked his head and observed the rigid person

doing her best imitation of a statue. Was this the same woman who'd danced for thirty minutes straight without a breather? Hard to believe.

For the sake of that memorable night, he dared to try again. "I don't mean to butt in, but I've noticed a few disgruntled glances among my coworkers. They're wonderful people, and I'd hate for them to get the wrong impression of—"

"I fully comprehend your point, Mr. Zimmerman." Victoria removed the glasses from her pert nose and focused on him. "Let me be clear. I intend to spend this semester doing the best job I possibly can, and I expect those around me to respond with an equal amount of excellence. If anyone finds my expectations threatening, they need to adjust their attitudes."

An alarm on her smartwatch beeped. She silenced it and gathered the remains of her lunch. "If you'll pardon me, I have work to do."

Andrew blinked. His lips hung useless, no words escaping.

He liked Victoria.

But it appeared Ronnie was right.

Principal Park was a harpy.

Chapter Five

The modest duplex sat back from the road, partially blocked from view by a gigantic oak tree. Victoria drove her borrowed clunker around the circular drive and pulled behind a small, white car. Her new neighbor must be home. She parked and surveyed the temporary lodgings. How had her luxury-apartment-loving brother lived here for over a year? From what she understood, Katherine had occupied the other side. Perhaps that's what drove them together.

The tempting trap of proximity.

She stepped from the car then dragged her carry-on from the back seat. A larger suitcase rested in the trunk, but she was too tired to retrieve it. After making the rounds to greet every employee in the school, her socializing battery was at negative percent. Her introverted self craved a quiet evening with a good book and a cup of hot tea.

After wheeling her suitcase up the sidewalk, Victoria climbed the front stoop and studied the two doors. Ryan neglected to say which side of the duplex was hers. She rattled the keys in her hand.

"Eeny, meeny, miny, moe." She pointed back and forth, landing on the door to her left. Walking forward, she knocked, but there was no answer. Victoria fit the key in the lock. It turned.

Hallelujah!

About time something went right. She pushed the front door open and entered the small living room. It was sparse but clean. A brown leather couch sat against the wall across from a flat-screen TV. Past a doorway stretched a decent-sized kitchen.

Too bad she didn't cook.

Barking sounded. Two black, furry bodies raced down the hallway and careened around her legs. One wore a tiny pink bow in its hair.

Weren't these Ryan and Katherine's dogs? What were their names? Romeo and Juliet?

No.

Not Juliet. Bella.

Romeo and Bella.

Victoria crouched to pick up the less squirmy puppy, held Romeo close to her face, and looked him in the eye. "What are you doing here? Did my brother bamboozle me into dog-sitting?"

Romeo's tiny tongue poked out and licked the tip of her nose.

She chuckled and scratched him on the head. "I wasn't counting on roommates."

The puppy's sister pawed at Victoria's pants. She hopped on her hind legs and barked.

"Bella!" A cheerful, male voice hollered from the back. "What's the problem?"

Victoria's body tightened. Romeo squirmed in her grasp. She rose and dug in her purse with her free hand.

Wait. Her pepper spray was packed in the suitcase.

Andrew Zimmerman appeared from the back hallway. Dressed in blue sweatpants and a loose, white T-shirt, he didn't spot her right away as he ruffled his wet hair with a towel. With joyous yips, Bella spun at his bare feet.

"I told y'all to keep the noise down," he chided. "We're getting a new neighbor soon. Whoever it is won't—"

He zeroed in on Victoria's high heels. Andrew froze. A shocked brown eye peeked out from the towel.

"Vic ... I mean ... Principal Park."

She clasped the puppy to her chest. "I'm sorry. I didn't realize ... I thought this was my apartment. The key. It fit in the door."

"I see." Andrew lowered the towel. "I guess Ryan didn't warn you. They put the same locks on both apartments. The key fits either one."

Her New Yorker instincts flinched. The same key for two separate apartments? How could anyone be that laissez-faire about tenant safety?

She cleared her throat. "It appears Ryan didn't warn you either. I'm your new neighbor."

ANDREW WRAPPED THE TOWEL AROUND HIS NECK AND HELD ON TO the ends. He eyed Victoria from the top of her immaculate hairdo to the tips of her shiny shoes. She stood as prim and proper as a character in a Jane Austen movie. He resisted the urge to ...

To what?

He didn't even know. If he'd found out yesterday that his attractive, Macarena-loving wedding partner lived next door, he'd have danced a jig in the church aisle on Sunday. But that was before the woman's ill-will tour through Sweetheart Elementary.

He balked at enduring her domineering ways for eight hours a day and then coming home to the same treatment. Would she inspect the property? Insist he mow the front lawn? Demand assigned parking spots?

On second thought, the unflagging optimist in him believed Victoria was in there somewhere under the pinstripes and bluster. Was it worth his time to search her out?

His gaze dropped to Romeo, the shier half of the puppy pair. The dog nestled in his neighbor's arms as her slender fingers gently stroked his fur. She appeared to do so without thought.

Her casual but caring act settled it in Andrew's mind.

The fun, warmhearted woman on the dance floor hadn't been an illusion. She still existed. Somewhere. And she needed help. Because the next five months would be intolerable for all of them if Victoria continued on the overbearing course she'd started. He owed it to her, his coworkers, and himself to show her a better path.

And he knew just how to start.

Chapter Six

A cacophony of car horns trumpeted as Victoria stood at her office window. She observed the morning drop-off procedure with mounting trepidation. The lengthy line of vehicles had begun in a deceptively quiet way. Early parents drove to the front of the building. Two aides in their early twenties opened the car doors and helped the children to the ground.

But as the start time for the school day drew closer, it devolved into a messy, aggressive sham. Tardy cars sped in a side entrance and cut into line. The people behind them blared their horns with angry fervor. Parents put their emergency lights on, got out of their cars, and kissed little ones goodbye, uncaring that they blocked the others from leaving.

Victoria's fists clenched. Her feet twitched inside her shoes, but she forced herself to remain in place. She couldn't fix this in one day.

But fix it she would.

The clamor. The attitudes. The lack of safety.

It hurt to witness the chaos. Good thing organization was

her forte. She'd design a plan to help bring order and easy solutions for everyone.

A knock sounded on the door.

"Come in," Victoria called without turning around.

"Good morning."

She recognized the upbeat, masculine voice. It belonged to her surprise next-door neighbor. She'd extricated herself from the awkward predicament last night with a quick apology and a quicker exit.

Many years as an apartment dweller taught her a polite but impersonal relationship between residents was best. And interrupting someone's shower was about as personal as it got. From this moment forward, she'd do her best to keep her distance from the man, even if he lived in the same duplex.

A delightful scent reached her nose. If she closed her eyes, it might be easy to imagine herself in the corner café of her New York neighborhood. A strong hand presented a tall paper cup in front of her face.

She popped off the plastic lid and sniffed the dark, rich aroma. "Is this espresso?"

She looked at Andrew, who held a matching cup to his own mouth. In his other hand, he held a cardboard carrier with one more coffee.

He finished a large gulp. "Yep. At the reception, you mentioned liking it."

Her insides cringed at the very mention of that night. If she'd returned to university life after the wedding, she could have treasured the remembrance of her impulsive kiss with the handsome groomsman. A sweet, flirtatious aberration. Now she couldn't dissociate the pleasant memories from the subsequent embarrassment.

Victoria concentrated on the coffee and took a sip. Her eyes opened wide. She drank deep, almost inhaling the robust brew.

"Wow." She downed a tasty shot. "This is better than my favorite place in the Village. Where did you get it?"

He smirked. "Sweetheart has hidden charms you know naught of."

She allowed herself a brief instant to savor the pungent brew. Bitter and sweet swirled together in a tantalizing combination. It tingled on her tongue and warmed her throat as she swallowed.

"It's amazing. You'll have to introduce me to the barista."

"With pleasure."

She smiled at him a full three seconds before remembering her vow to keep her distance. Turning to the window, she pointed at the outside havoc. "Is it always this bad?"

He sighed. "Just the last ten minutes. Some drivers forget their manners in their rush to avoid sign-in."

She set the coffee on her nearby desk and grabbed a pen. "Sign-in?"

Andrew nodded. "Anyone who arrives after 7:51 a.m. has to take their kids to the office and sign them in. If parents are already late for work, they don't want to add an extra five minutes."

"Why don't they just leave earlier?"

"Glory be!" He pressed a hand to his chest in faux surprise. "Why didn't we think of that? You've solved the whole problem."

Victoria responded through clenched teeth. "Don't you have young minds to mold?"

"The homeroom teachers take attendance first." He glanced at his watch. "There's still a good twelve minutes, if you need help with anything."

"I do." She scribbled on a notepad. "Why are there only two aides helping with the car line?"

He shrugged. "It's been the procedure since I started

working here. Sweetheart subscribes to the age-old tradition: if it ain't broke, don't fix it."

"And how bad does it have to get before the town considers something"—she kept her head bent but disdain saturated her voice—"broke?"

A car horn bellowed as if to punctuate her point.

Andrew hesitated. "Please accept this comment in the friendly spirit it's intended. You should keep in mind, folks around here are slow to accept change. I'm trying to help you settle into the job with as little trouble as possible."

"Thanks for the tip"—she gifted him with her most courteous smile—"and the espresso."

"Victoria." He moved closer.

"Mr. Zimmerman." She took a step back. "I'd appreciate if you called me Ms. Park whenever we're on campus."

"Ms. Park?" His brows rose in a disbelieving arch. "You're serious? We're the only people in the room."

Victoria spun on her heel. She walked around the desk, moved to the door, and opened it, her fingers resting on the handle. "Whether there are two people or two hundred, I believe in maintaining professional boundaries at work."

In the hallway, a teacher walked backwards, calling instructions to her line of students. The woman cast a glance inside the office as she passed. Andrew crossed the room and lowered his voice.

"I know the culture at Sweetheart Elementary, *Ms. Park.* The principal you're replacing was a kind, understanding woman who held the reins with a firm but gentle hand. I imagine the staff feel this place is good enough the way it is."

Victoria's lips thinned in a tense line. "I intend to devote my heart and soul to improving this school. An almost-collision in a parking lot where children are present is not acceptable, and anyone who's resistant to change will need to open their mind to my modifications. *Good enough* isn't good enough anymore." She proffered a hand at the hallway. "Have a nice day, Mr. Zimmerman."

ANDREW STARED AT THE DOOR SHE HAD SHUT IN HIS FACE.

Have a nice day?

Was she an airline stewardess?

He'd arrived at school with the espresso peace offering in hand, hoping to sweet-talk her into enjoying coffee with Ronnie and him in the main office. The secretary was the key to the school. If he could just get Victoria to see that.

Correction. Principal Park.

If the stubborn woman wouldn't listen to reason, he'd insist. Andrew raised a fist to pound on the barrier between them and planned to use a less subtle delivery with his advice this time.

"Hey, Mr. Z!" A young boy with sparkling brown eyes and jet-black hair ran to hug him. The student rotated around his body with arms encasing Andrew's legs.

Andrew deleted the frustration from his expression. "Hey, Mateo. Why aren't you in class?"

"My teacher let me get a drink of water." He continued spinning.

"I see." Andrew ruffled the dark hair. "Get back before your friends miss you."

"Awwww." His mouth folded into a frown. "Can't I stay with you?"

"Nope. My first class is with pre-K. You're too grown up for their stuff."

"I guess." Mateo turned in the direction of his classroom,

making sure to wander with slow, meandering steps all the way there.

Andrew resisted the urge to hurry the boy. He'd get there eventually. Might as well let him work off some energy first.

He eyed the closed door and reconsidered confronting the new principal. Perhaps God had sent a tiny, hyperactive angel to delay his impulsive plan. What good would it do to give Victoria Park an earful? With her imperious manner, she must consider everyone in Sweetheart a bunch of hicks.

Too bad he'd wasted his money on the pricey espresso. Next time, she could drink the break room sludge like everyone else. And forget paving her way with the locals. When Victoria found herself in over her head, she'd better not run to him for help.

Chapter Seven

A scream erupted.

Victoria bolted straight up in bed and threw the covers off. Was someone in her apartment? She reached to the bedside table for her pepper spray. Her hand knocked into the alarm clock. Unidentified items fell to the floor with a clatter.

Another cry. This time, her sleep-fogged brain processed the sound. It wasn't screaming. It was crowing.

A rooster.

"You've got to be kidding." She moaned.

Reaching to the carpet, she fumbled in the darkness for the things she'd knocked over and set the digital clock on the nightstand.

3:02 a.m.

Didn't roosters crow when the sun came up? Why was this one ahead of schedule?

It had taken her forever to fall asleep. Something in the Sweetheart air didn't agree with her sinuses, and a stuffy nose–headache combo left her restless. This was not the morning for a hillbilly wake-up call.

The bird shrieked again, so loud the noise hurt her ears like it was right outside the window behind her bed. Victoria leaned over the headboard and yanked the curtains back. Two beady yellow eyes met hers.

"Aaaaaaah!" She scrambled backward.

The rooster stared through the glass. Its black feathers stuck on end, and the blue comb atop its head wavered. Blue!

Why was a punk rocker chicken peeping in her window at three in the morning?

She sat on her knees and shooed her hands. "Go away."

He glared at her. His scrawny head bounced. The rooster opened its beak and released a chorus of unamused screeches.

Could this bird belong to Andrew? She'd text him, but they'd never exchanged numbers. Grabbing her velvet robe from the foot of her bed, she slipped her feet into slippers and plodded through the living room, out of her apartment, and to her neighbor's front door.

The porch light cast a golden glow in the darkness. Perhaps she should wait until later. An unbroken stillness enveloped her. Not so much as a car horn. The whole town must be asleep.

Except her.

Raucous crowing sounded from the rear of the house. The rooster and her.

Victoria knocked. No answer. She knocked harder.

A few seconds later, a barely awake Andrew opened the door. Honey-brown hair stuck up in a wavy half mohawk. The indention from a pillow creased his left cheek.

Looking down with a glazed expression, he reminded her of a sleepy little boy. Teaching was hard work. Would he be able to fall asleep again? The rudeness of her early morning visit hit her.

"I apologize for waking you, Mr. Zimmerman. Do you know who owns that bird?"

"Bird?" His unfocused gaze wandered around the porch. "What bird?"

"The rooster in the backyard. He's crowing his head off like he's determined to wake the sun three hours ahead of schedule."

He yawned and rubbed a hand over his drowsy face. "Oh, that's Old Blue."

"A fitting moniker," she droned.

Andrew laughed. "You get used to him. Normally, he stays closer to the back of the property. I guess he was checking out the new tenant."

"Does he belong to you?"

"Nope. The lady with the house behind us owns Blue. Sometimes you can't hear him, but he hops the fence on occasion and crows up a storm, marking his territory. The old codger wants us to realize who's boss."

"I see." Victoria stepped away from the door. "Thank you for telling me. Good night."

"I think you mean *good morning*. School starts in less than" —Andrew ducked his head in the house, presumably to check the clock—"four hours. I hope this day goes smoother for you."

"Smoother?" She cocked her head. "I assumed the first day was successful. Apart from the atrocious car line situation. And I intend to address the issue at our staff meeting after school."

"You discovered a solution?"

"It's simple. If we rotate the teachers to help with drop-off instead of everyone waiting for their classes in the gym, we'll have more hands to open car doors."

"Oh, they'll love that suggestion."

～

ANDREW TRIED TO KEEP THE SARCASM FROM HIS TONE BUT DIDN'T totally succeed. Did the woman possess zero self-awareness? Since her first workday on campus, when she'd thrown her authoritative weight around, the staff avoided her. Any changes she made were sure to be met with hostility. But forcing the teachers to open car doors like hotel valets?

They might mutiny.

Victoria stood in a full-length robe, posture straight as an etiquette coach's. She probably had no clue she still wore a bright green nasal strip on the bridge of her nose.

His lips twitched, and he studied his bare feet. Composing himself, he met her gaze. "It's a logical plan, however, I suspect you may encounter pushback."

She quirked an eyebrow. "From what I observed yesterday morning, most teachers congregate around the gym, chatting and drinking coffee. There are more than enough people inside. If half of them monitor the children after they arrive and the rest help on the car line, we'll be able to service the parents much faster."

Andrew crossed the threshold. "Please don't take what I'm about to say the wrong way." His toes crinkled on the cold porch concrete. "You're an outsider. Insisting the teachers add more to their plates, right at the start of the day, will not go down well. It's already an exhausting job, and you want to increase their load."

She met his challenge with a lifted chin. "I assure you I will not ask any more from them than I do from myself. I intend to be right there on the line each morning, starting tomorrow. Safety trumps socializing with colleagues."

Andrew placed one bare foot on top of the other to avoid the chill. Maybe he'd follow his coworkers' example and run the opposite direction whenever Victoria came in sight. Why was she dead set on doing things her way?

Blue let out another ear-piercing cry.

It looked like the rooster wasn't the only one marking his territory.

Chapter Eight

Victoria checked her hair in the small mirror on the office wall. She'd swept the thick, black locks into a French twist. Her ivory silk blouse and tailored pencil skirt offered a softer appearance than her previous black suit. Even her shoes were low pumps instead of the usual four-inch heels. She'd bought this outfit for a New York luncheon honoring an influential politician. Would the understated but elegant couture overwhelm the locals?

She wanted to project a gentler image to the teachers. Her new morning drop-off plan would be unveiled at the after-school staff meeting, and she needed every psychological benefit available. Until then, she'd spend a quiet day catching up on paperwork.

A brisk knock, and the secretary entered without waiting for permission. What was her name again? Lana? Lonnie?

Ronnie.

"Good morning, Ronnie." Victoria turned on a friendly smile.

"I doubt it." The towering woman shoved a piece of paper

at her. "We've had three teachers and two staff call in sick. I figure the flu is going around."

Victoria took the list and read the names. "Are there enough people to cover the classes?"

"All but one." Ronnie scratched the back of her skull. "And it's a doozy. Pre-K."

"Isn't there a temp service to call for a substitute?"

The secretary laughed. "This ain't the big city. We don't have a professional agency with a pool of ready-made substitutes. I already called everyone I know to watch the older classes. No one will take pre-K."

Victoria tilted her head. "Could you do it?"

"I could." Ronnie nodded. "But I won't. I raised and graduated four of my own. My time with babies and crying is over. I've done my duty. Besides"—she pointed at the list in Victoria's hand—"one of the sick staff members is the other secretary. Someone has to cover the front office."

Victoria walked around her desk. "Then the solution is simple. I'll cover pre-K."

"Excuse me?" Ronnie leaned an ear closer.

"It's not an ideal solution." She drew a pair of tennis shoes from the bag under her desk and slipped off her dress pumps. "But I used to babysit when I was in high school. I imagine there's not much difference. Is there a schedule for the children?"

As Victoria laced her sneakers, Ronnie listed everything from naps and outdoor play to snack time. Victoria looked at her outfit and suppressed a moan. Of all days to choose a cream ensemble. Oh well. She'd be careful.

The air conditioner kicked on. A cold draft tickled the nape of her neck like an icy finger. Or a warning. Ronnie might see a confident problem-solver before her, but doubts flooded Victoria's mind.

Could she do this?

Two hours later, she had her answer.

"No!"

An angry red face stared at Victoria. The little girl's brown hair flopped as she shook her head for the fifth time. Her dimpled, chubby cheeks might have been adorable if they weren't screwing up to let loose another unearthly howl.

The child screamed and plopped her rear end on the rainbow-colored rug.

Victoria shifted the crying boy she was holding to the other hip and reached for the four-year-old.

"No. No. Noooooooooooooo!" She crawled away.

Two girls banged wooden blocks against the plastic kitchen setup in the corner. A group of children sat coloring, the crayons streaking from their papers to the table underneath. The child in her arms buried his face in the crook of her shoulder. Wet tears dripped onto her silk collar, and a suspicious wetness met the hand propped under his bottom.

Yes. Cream was definitely the wrong choice for today.

Victoria lifted desperate eyes to the ceiling and prayed.

Please, Lord, let dismissal come quickly!

ANDREW SETTLED ON A BENCH IN THE LUNCHROOM WITH ELBOWS resting on the table. This Tuesday felt more like a Monday— dragging on and on. The early morning altercation with his aggravated neighbor hadn't helped. After hearing her ill-advised plans for drop-off, he'd laid in bed staring at the ceiling. Missing three hours of sleep made the workday interminable. But it was almost over. If he could stay awake through the staff meeting.

His coworkers chatted as they waited for Principal Park to

arrive. He checked the clock. She was three minutes late. Very unusual.

A squeak sounded from the teacher on his right. He followed her gaze to the entrance where Victoria strode through the cafeteria doorway, a stack of papers in hand. She wore a cream outfit, swanky except for the wrinkled blouse and messy red handprint on the skirt's hem. Tufts of hair bulged from the sides of her updo. A dark-black bruise adorned her left calf.

What happened?

With chin held high, Victoria stopped in front of the group and adjusted the lopsided neck of her silk top. "I apologize for being late. I didn't get a chance to make copies until after dismissal." She handed the stack to the person on her left. "Please pass these around while I explain the improvements we'll be implementing to our morning drop-off procedure."

She spent ten minutes detailing her open, assist, keep-them-moving brainstorm then switched to the dress code. Her announcement that teachers would only be allowed to wear jeans on casual Fridays caused a collective gasp.

Victoria paused and reviewed her paper. "I realize this is a sacrifice. However, it's one worth making. We must maintain the standard we want to develop in the children. If we look great, it will inspire them to look great." She gave a self-conscious tug to her hand-print-stained skirt. "I've had firsthand experience with the effort it takes to care for the children. I'm not asking you to wear dress clothes. But please save the jeans for Fridays. Maintain a high standard."

Her motivational speech went over about as well as Andrew expected. Not at all. She asked for questions at the end of her presentation, and stony silence answered.

Victoria thanked everyone for coming, dismissed them, and exited the room without speaking to anyone. Grumbles abounded as the teachers left the cafeteria. Andrew stared at the empty spot where Principal Park had stood. Part of him wanted to check on her, but he remembered his pledge to leave Victoria to her own devices.

He rose and headed for the door, then met Ronnie in the hallway.

"How was your day?" he asked.

"Crazy!" She rubbed her temples. "The staff shortage kept us hopping. If Ms. Park hadn't covered pre-K, we wouldn't have made it."

"I'm sorry." Andrew leaned forward. "Did you say pre-K?"

"I underestimated her." Ronnie blew out a breath. "The girl may be full of vinegar, but she's a tough one. Stuck it out until dismissal and didn't call for help once." Her cell phone rang. She answered, gave him a wave, and left.

Andrew dragged his weary body to collect his things. He passed the pre-K classroom and glanced inside. If he was tired, Victoria must be worn out.

Toys littered the floor. Crayon marks covered the tabletops. Tiny red handprints dotted the back wall.

Andrew chuckled. His wedding partner had experienced the elementary version of a trial by fire. It took guts to watch the babies. He dreaded the forty minutes he spent with them in music once a week. Yet, their principal lasted a whole day.

Victoria Park possessed hidden depths. What kind of woman was able to marshal a car line, tend a roomful of tumultuous toddlers, and dance the Macarena with abandon?

What had Ronnie said? Full of vinegar but tough. His favorite kind of potato chips were salt and vinegar.

Andrew grinned then shook his head. *No can do.* He'd better be careful, or he'd find himself chasing a lady who was sure to shut him down at every turn.

Chapter Nine

Thunder rumbled as Victoria exited the school building with a megaphone in hand. She hoped the weather wasn't foreshadowing her morning. Today couldn't be as bad as yesterday.

At least there were no crying children.

Operation Car Line Makeover was a go. Her handout at the after-school staff meeting had detailed the practical ways they would fix the traffic flow problem. She'd spent three hours creating a schedule that rotated the teachers so they only had car line duty twice a week.

Where were the teachers anyway?

Checking behind her, Victoria saw reluctant bodies trudging through the double doors. She tightened the laces on her sneakers and stood straight. Pressing the megaphone button, it squealed as she began to speak.

"Please spread out. Two car spaces apart. Open one door and immediately move to the next."

Victoria checked the line, adjusting a few teachers to the proper distance. Passing a large oak tree by the sidewalk, she nearly tripped on an iron grill sticking out of the pavement.

She examined the water drainage grate. The rusty metal teeth bent up from the concrete ditch like a lawsuit waiting to happen. She pulled her phone from her pocket, took a picture, and made a note to alert the maintenance man. Students could seriously hurt themselves.

A blustery breeze kicked up. The cars started to arrive in a slow trickle. Teachers at the line's end stood unoccupied, shifting their weight from one foot to another.

Victoria popped the handle of a pickup truck. "Good morning," she singsonged, helping the young girl from the high seat before hurrying to the next car. "Good morning," she repeated after opening a new door.

A small boy in a T-shirt, jeans, and cowboy boots hopped outside and threw his arms around her legs. "Hi."

"Um, hello." Her hands froze at waist level. Did she know this child? Had she met him at the wedding?

He stared at her with sloped eyebrows. "Who are you?"

"I-I'm the new principal, Ms. Park."

"Oh. Okay." He released her, grabbed a backpack from inside the car, and walked away.

Victoria shut the door. Maybe it was a Southern thing. She'd heard they were friendlier than New Yorkers.

The traffic increased, and everyone scurried. Teachers helped the students from the cars, but there were still parents holding up the line with their three-minute kisses, hair bow fixing, and picture-taking routines. She rolled her eyes to the stormy clouds overhead. The drivers would see their children in a matter of hours. Why was a full-on goodbye ceremony necessary?

Victoria spoke into the megaphone. "Move down, please." She waved her hand toward the exit with the courtesy of a Broadway theater usher. "Move down, please!"

She checked her watch.

7:43.

This was about the time it grew crazy. When the tardy people zoomed in from the side entrance. But not anymore.

Victoria observed the barrier of orange plastic cones she'd placed to block the alternate turn-in. Today, there would be no cutting in line.

A horn sounded. In the back, a red sports car skipped the line and swerved into the wrong lane, where cars were supposed to exit. Victoria raced across the parking lot and stood in front of the car. A woman with a hot pink, floral scarf around her hair glared from the front seat.

Victoria raised her megaphone with a friendly, "I'm sorry, ma'am. Please put your vehicle in reverse and get in line."

The driver laid on the horn. It blared at Victoria, but she kept her smile in place. Pointing her outstretched arm at the street, she nodded her head.

Tires squealed as the woman backed out. Black marks decorated the pavement.

A tiny thrill of victory coursed through Victoria's veins. Fairness won. Order had prevailed.

She hurried to the line, stood at the head, and studied the procedure.

Victoria drew in a deep breath. She loved the smell of efficiency in the morning. The alarm on her watch buzzed.

"Okay, people. It's 7:50. Get ready!"

"Excuse me, Ms. Park? I have a question." Ms. Amy, a timid young teacher she recognized from pre-K, beckoned to her. "What do we do?"

"Finish opening these doors and get the clipboards. Anyone after the 7:51 cut-off will have to sign in."

Victoria motioned the finished cars forward and took a clipboard from a pile on the sidewalk as the new drivers pulled up.

She opened a car door and passed it to the man behind the wheel. "Good morning, can you please sign the tardy sheet?"

"What?" He stared at the clipboard in confusion. "I'm already here."

"Yes, sir. But it's 7:51. Anyone who hasn't dropped their child off by now is officially late."

"What kind of crazy rule is that?" His hairy eyebrows knotted in a furry line.

"The state of Texas requires public schools to sign in any students who arrive after the designated time."

A little girl with freckles dusting her nose sat on the seat beside him. No booster seat or safety belt. The man obviously didn't care about state regulations.

He slapped the steering wheel. "My kid has gone here for two years. We've never signed in before."

Victoria made sure to keep a kind, if somewhat vapid, smile in place as if she couldn't hear the contempt in his tone. What she wanted to say was, *Your free ride is over, pal*. But she didn't.

"I understand this might be unfamiliar. We're making these changes to keep the drop-off line safe for the children and help parents get through quicker. That's why we brought clipboards. To save you from having to park and walk in the office."

He muttered under his breath but signed the list. Victoria helped the girl out of the car and held her backpack while she slipped her arms through the straps. The student hurried to the school entrance, and Victoria took the clipboard from the dad.

"Thank you, sir. Have a wonderful morning."

She shut the door. He drove away with an extra engine rev to punctuate his displeasure. Glancing down the line, Victoria noted several teachers struggling to obtain signatures. She hurried to where Ms. Amy stood at a red sports car, shoulders hunched almost to her ears. Behind the wheel sat the woman with the floral scarf.

Uh-oh. The line cutter.

Victoria took the clipboard from Ms. Amy's shaking hand. "I'll take care of this family. Why don't you go inside and gather your class?"

The young teacher's watery eyes glowed with gratitude just before she dashed away.

Victoria bent at the passenger side's open window. The mother glared at her, hands with bulging knuckles grasping the steering wheel. A familiar little girl with black curls sat beside her.

"I remember you." Victoria waved at her. "We met at the wedding. What was your name?"

"Sophie," she said.

"Hello again, Sophie." Victoria turned her attention to the mother. "Good morning, ma'am. I'd be happy to escort your daughter inside if you'll please sign her in." She held out the clipboard.

"I'm not signing that." The woman put her car in Park and crossed her arms. "I'll sit here all day if I have to before I bow to your power trip."

Look who's talking about power trips.

Victoria slipped the pen underneath the clip. "I assure you, I take no pleasure in confrontation. Please feel free to keep your child with you. I'll ask the office to mark her absent. Have a nice day."

"Wuuu—"

She walked away but spun on her heel when she heard the engine start and the door open. Victoria sped to the car and found Sophie halfway out.

Victoria bent once more to face the mother. "And just in case you've decided to leave your daughter on the sidewalk and drive away, she will be taken straight to the office, where she'll stay until you return and sign her in. I'd hate to waste your day." Victoria held out the clipboard with a smile. "This really is the easiest way."

ANDREW SCOURED HIS HOUSE FOR A MISSING FLASH DRIVE. HE'D USED it in December to save the holiday program soundtracks. Who knew where it disappeared? Peeking under the bed, he found a half-eaten bag of peanuts. He made his way to the hallway closet and opened the door. Boxes piled to the ceiling. And he hadn't missed whatever they contained. A large, black case in the back caught his eye.

His cello.

He couldn't remember the last time he'd played it.

That was a lie.

Andrew knew the exact concert when he'd last held the bow. He rubbed the tips of his fingers. The calluses he'd built up over years of daily practice were starting to soften. How long before they were gone entirely?

He shut the door. Passing the living room window, Andrew stopped as Victoria's car parked in the driveway. She climbed from the ancient sedan and stumbled to the porch steps, her hands full of file folders, with a purse swinging from one arm and a briefcase from the other. She'd kept the sneakers on all day. Small wonder after the way her morning started.

His classroom window overlooked the parking lot. He'd been glued to the outside drama during sign-in. Principal Park's new policy didn't gel with the natives. When he'd worked as a substitute teacher in Austin, the practice was a normal part of school life. But after moving to Sweetheart, he'd quickly discovered they used a more laid-back approach with tardies. A "that's okay, honey; we all run late sometimes" system.

But Victoria had won herself a fan in Ms. Amy. The shy, young pre-K teacher, fresh out of college, jumped at loud noises, and the confrontational car line must have been torture. After Principal Park took her place, facing one of the most belligerent parents in the school, Ms. Amy looked at her like she were a knight in shining armor or whatever the female equivalent was.

One thing about Victoria. She didn't create a plan and leave the minions to deal with the consequences. She dove right in the trenches with them.

The timer dinged. He headed for the kitchen, grabbed a pot holder, and opened the oven door, the sweet scent of meatloaf drifting from inside. Would Victoria accept a friendly meal? It was worth an attempt. He fixed a plate with an extra helping of veggies for his neighbor. Her tactics might be abrasive and her personality bullheaded, but she still needed to eat. Andrew headed out to the porch and knocked on her front door.

After a few seconds, Victoria opened it. She appeared much shorter without her high heels, the top of her head reaching to his shoulder.

He held the plate out with straight arms. "I think you've earned this."

She snatched the dinner and held it to her nose. "Oh my word. Thank you."

He bit back a laugh at her enthusiasm. She hadn't turned him down. A minor victory.

He smirked. "Sure you don't want to save it for later?"

"No chance." Her weary eyes gazed at him. "I don't have enough strength to open the fridge, let alone cook."

"Rough day?"

"To say the least." She stretched her bare foot in a circle. "I may never fit my toes in a pair of heels again. Why is everything a battle in Sweetheart?"

"Maybe because you always come dressed in your armor."

Victoria glared.

He held up both hands. "Sorry. I admire your tenacity. When you see a problem, you try to fix it. A praiseworthy habit. Even if there are easier ways to approach people with your suggestions."

She sighed. "If you're going to lecture me, come in and sit at the table. At least I can eat while you do it."

Andrew followed her into the apartment that used to be occupied by her sister-in-law before Katherine's marriage. He'd helped the newlyweds move most of her stuff to their new home. The remaining furniture and bare setup were the same as he remembered. It appeared Victoria hadn't added so much as a picture or vase of flowers.

He cocked an eyebrow her way. "Nice personal touches."

She waved him to the kitchen with the hand not holding her plate. "I know you're being sarcastic, but I'm too exhausted to think of a response."

He took pity on her and dropped the subject. She found silverware in the drawer, they settled at the table, and Victoria tasted her first bite of meatloaf. She immediately took another.

Andrew watched her dig into the pile of mashed potatoes. "What brings you home at this hour? Most of us left school by five o'clock."

She swallowed. "I noticed some students were waiting at drop-off much longer than others. I checked with the teachers, and it seems to be an epidemic. Parents treat them like free babysitters while they finish their errands. I remained with them and informed the late arrivals there would now be a two-dollar charge for every ten minutes they keep the teachers waiting."

"How did that go over?"

She ate another bite of meatloaf. "Pushback from both sides. The parents didn't appreciate paying for their mistakes, and the teachers preferred not making waves." She moaned. "Why can't people believe I want to help?"

Andrew remained silent. Pointing out her pushy way of helping wouldn't be appreciated. Better to wait for the right opportunity. He required an opening.

Victoria finished the last bite of her dinner and pushed the plate away. "What would I have done without your assistance? Probably starved." She offered him a grateful smile. "How can I repay you?"

Hello, opening.

Andrew hesitated. She'd treated him with a friendlier attitude than he'd seen from her since the wedding. He shouldn't risk it, but he hated for her to suffer.

He drummed his fingers on the table. "You could let me assist in different ways."

She slumped against her chair. "How do you mean?"

"It wasn't too many months ago I was a newcomer to Sweetheart myself."

Victoria stared. "But you fit in so well. I thought you were born here."

"Nope. I'm glad I blend in with my adopted home. It didn't come naturally." He gestured to her almost-empty plate. "I didn't even know how to make meatloaf until Ronnie taught me."

"When did you move to Sweetheart?"

"It's been a little over a year."

"Just a year?" Victoria sat up. "You seem like a local."

"Thanks. Believe it or not, it took a while to adjust to the slower pace of things. I can give you a few tips on small-town culture." He held his breath, expecting a rejection.

Victoria didn't answer right away. She picked up her silverware, piled them on the plate, and folded her hands on the table.

Oh boy. Was he about to get skewered by Principal Park? Again?

Chapter Ten

Day two of Operation Car Line Makeover was shaping up to be worse than the first. A new rotation of teachers had taken their positions with resentful expressions. Several congregated underneath the huge oak tree by the sidewalk to avoid the glare of the rising sun. Andrew understood their frustration. Being a teacher presented enough challenges without adding a soul-sapping confrontation with parents to their morning.

Number one item on the agenda: set a positive tone, for everyone's sake. He smiled at the tardy cars like he was greeting his best friend.

After approaching a black SUV, he tucked the clipboard under his arm and swung the door open. *"You're late, late, late."* Andrew sang the words in the deep tone of a sixties doo-wopper. *"I couldn't wait, wait, wait."* He pointed finger guns at the boy climbing out. *"To see you, you, you. Boo-hoo-hoo, hoo, hoo."* He rubbed his fists over his eyes.

The mother behind the wheel laughed. "You're a trip, Mr. Z."

Andrew offered the clipboard. *"So please sign, sign, sign. On the line, line, line. It's a pain, pain, pain.*" He waggled a finger. "*But don't complain, plain, plain.*"

She scribbled on the tardy sheet and passed it back. "Will I get a new song if I'm late tomorrow?"

He faked a snooty tone. "Tomorrow, I may try opera."

His ditty worked on everybody except the parent with the chest-length beard in the black monster truck with red flames painted on the sides. The father argued, swore, and threatened to call the school board. Andrew kept his cool and obtained the signature from him after promising to report the man's displeasure to the office as soon as the car line finished.

He swung by Ronnie's desk to drop off the clipboard. "We had an unhappy customer who desires every single person in administration to be informed how much he dislikes the new sign-in procedure. His name was"—he checked the list—"Mr. Crumm."

Ronnie chortled. "That last name. I never get used to it, no matter how many times I hear it."

"Well, Mr. Crumm had a crummy attitude today." Andrew tapped the clipboard. "It almost took bloodshed for me to get this signature. Please have someone send an email stating his complaint has been received. I don't want him driving his monster truck through my classroom window."

He gave Ronnie a wink and turned as Victoria walked through the front entrance with a stack of clipboards in hand. *Marched* would be a better description. The Parks must have a brigadier general somewhere in their family tree. She wore another black pinstripe ensemble. How many did she have? This one was a suit coat and skirt set with a matching blouse. Did she own any outfits in a color other than black or white? Her hair was pulled into a tight, no-nonsense bun to match her tight, no-nonsense attitude.

Dinner last night had left him feeling kindlier to his prickly next-door neighbor. As a teacher, he hated to leave anyone in ignorance. Although she hadn't accepted his offer to explain the joys of small-town living, neither had she laughed in his face.

It was a start.

She struggled with her burden of tardy sign-ins, and his feet moved forward on automatic. He stopped. Experience warned she wouldn't appreciate his help. But something inside him always ached to assist the pretty principal.

VICTORIA BALANCED THE LOAD OF CUMBERSOME CLIPBOARDS IN HER hand. There must be a more efficient way to facilitate sign-in. Could they create name tags with scan codes? It would save the teachers and parents the trouble of papers and pens.

"Hi, Ms. Bark." One of the tardies, a redheaded girl with pigtails and two front teeth missing rushed through the door to hug her.

"It's Park," Victoria said.

"Huh?"

"My name is Ms. Park."

"Oh." She gave a gap-toothed grin. "Sorry." Her backpack dragged on the ground as she left to find her class.

"Ms. Bark?" An amused voice sounded behind Victoria. "Dare I say it suits you?"

She spun to find Andrew, arms crossed and a quiver on his lips, leaning against a column.

"Do you think she did it on purpose?" Victoria squinted at the child's back.

"Doubtful."

"I suppose I'll have to visit each classroom to introduce

myself in person. The students should pronounce my name properly."

"And do you know *her* name?" Andrew pointed in the direction the redhead disappeared.

"Two hundred thirty-eight students attend this institution, and I started working here three days ago. Of course I don't know her name."

"Then why are you so offended she doesn't know yours?"

Victoria raised her chin. "It's not the same thing. There's only one of me."

"That's for sure."

She regarded him with suspicion. If he meant his comment in a derogatory way, Andrew's innocent air didn't betray him. He gazed at her with a pleasant, unreadable expression.

Seconds ticked. The shrill bell rang through the hallway. Distant sounds of bodies scrambling and doors shutting filled the school.

"Repeat after me," he said. "Good morning, sweetie."

"I beg your pardon." Fire flooded her cheeks. Ice entered her tone. "I don't appreciate being called—"

"Remember my offer to help you assimilate to small-town ways? I'm trying to teach you how to interact with the children."

He hadn't been calling her *sweetie*. What was she thinking? Relief mixed with the tiniest shred of disappointment addled Victoria's already confused brain.

She relaxed a smidgen. "I didn't say *yes* to your offer."

"But you didn't say *no*. You just stared at me and put the dishes in the sink. I took that as silent consent." He smiled. "Come on. You can do it. Good morning, sweetie!"

"What kind of course is this? The Empathy Curriculum?"

"You might call it that. And the lessons are free. What a deal!" He placed a gentle hand at her elbow and propelled her to a nearby wooden bench along the wall. Guiding Victoria to a sitting position, he took the spot beside her. "A softer approach works well on children and adults alike. Even if you can't remember everyone's name, you can make them feel appreciated. If *sweetie* doesn't appeal to you, how about *honey* or *dear*?"

"I grew up in New York not the Deep South." She launched to her feet. "It's disingenuous for me to talk in such a manner."

"Fine." He joined her. "Pick a greeting that suits your jurisdiction. What terms of endearment do they use in the Big Apple?"

Victoria snorted. "Hey *you*?"

"Mmmmm." He scrunched his face. "While colorful, it's missing the sympathetic quality I was going for. Try injecting a touch of Southern into your salutations. Trust me. The kids won't judge you for it."

A crooked line of kindergartners, a few still finishing the last bites of their breakfast bagels, walked from the lunchroom. At the end of the line, the redhead with lopsided pigtails fell behind. She studied her arm intently as she passed.

Looking their way, the girl yanked on Victoria's skirt. "Miss Bark."

Victoria sighed. "Park."

"Huh?"

"Never mind." She pasted on a smile that was faker than the designer perfume they sold on the street by her father's apartment in Queens. "What do you need?"

Andrew cleared his throat.

She glanced over. He raised both eyebrows and mouthed something. Victoria tried to contain her eye roll.

"What do you need, sweetie?" she amended.

All the professors at her former university would cackle with glee if they saw her now. Especially the jerk who took her associate dean position. How many cringeworthy adjustments would she have to make to work with these younger scholars?

The redhead held up her arm. "I'm bleeding."

"What!" Victoria crouched. "Where?" She scanned the child from head to toe but couldn't find the injury.

"Here." She pointed to a tiny red dot.

"You don't"—Victoria resisted another eye roll—"you're not bleeding. It's just a little raw."

"Raw?"

"Yes. You must have scratched a scab. Please rejoin the line. Your class is leaving you."

The child's eyes widened. She backed away and hurried after her friends.

Victoria turned to find Andrew rubbing a hand over his face.

"What?" she said. "I called her sweetie."

"Yes. You did." He patted her shoulder. "As I tell the students, good job. If you'll excuse me, it's time for my first class."

Victoria studied his vibrating back as he walked away. She'd bet a month's pay he was laughing. Was this her reward for going along with the empathy lesson?

No more.

She headed for her office but paused when her foot telegraphed an unhappy message. Leaning on the front counter, Victoria checked her heel. It looked like she was a little raw too. She'd foregone the sneakers this morning. Now, her dress shoe had chafed her skin the color of an uncooked tenderloin.

"Mmmm-mmm-mmm." Ronnie wagged a finger from behind the desk. "That's what you get for wearing those fancy high heels. Why not invest in some comfortable, padded shoes?"

"I'd rather not." Victoria slipped her shoe on despite the pain. "As the principal, I must present a professional, put-together image to the parents. It saves time when you make a good impression from the get-go."

"Are you sure it's not your pride you're saving?" Ronnie puckered her mouth.

"I beg your pardon." Victoria rose as high as her five-foot-five-plus-heels stature allowed. "How is dressing in an appropriate manner prideful?"

"You know, sugar—"

"Ms. Park."

Ronnie studied her. "You know, *Ms. Park*, there are two kinds of pride. The regular kind is bad, when people brag about themselves, tilt their noses in the air, and refuse to admit when they're wrong. But then there's the sneaky kind, which is ten times worse. It makes you dress, talk, and act as if the whole world is banking on you. You always have to be perfect, because your pride says, 'I don't need any help. I can do it myself.' You depend on your own abilities and don't let anyone else offer a hand. Not even God. That's why sneaky pride is so dangerous."

Victoria suppressed the angry words flooding her brain. Was everyone in Sweetheart determined to educate her? Andrew tore down her social capabilities, and the school secretary lambasted her very core. Victoria's lips formed a pinched smile. "I'm afraid I must object to your psychological evaluation. There's nothing wrong with being a perfectionist."

"Don't take offense, sugar." Ronnie tapped the counter. "I speak as an expert, because I have firsthand experience in sneaky pride. It took me years to recognize it in myself, and I was hoping to save you a few mistakes I made. You might not be ready to hear it now. But one day, my words will make sense to you." The phone jingled at her elbow. She picked up the receiver. "Sweetheart Elementary, where we love 'em like they're our own. How can I help you?"

Victoria stalked to her office. Five months and three days until the semester ended and freed her from this tiny burg. She could remain civil and hold her tongue for that long.

But she wished the good citizens of Sweetheart would follow her example.

Chapter Eleven

Victoria took the sign-in sheets to her office and deposited them on her desk. Arguing with the parents took way too much time. There must be a more efficient way. She should research how the top elementary schools handled their drop-off procedures.

After creating a spreadsheet and entering the tardy parents' names, she spent two hours examining education blogs and school websites. A high-pitched shriek made her neck hairs stand on end. What now? Victoria raced to the door.

In the hallway, a little boy with blond curls sprawled on the floor. His feet churned like he was on a bicycle.

Andrew stood beside him, grasping a superhero action figure. "Micah, you can't bring toys to music class."

The unhappy student squirmed, chest heaving with noisy sobs, as his red T-shirt rolled halfway up his pudgy belly.

Victoria looked around, but no other teachers appeared. Weren't they alarmed by the noise? Someone might be dying.

Andrew crossed his arms. "Crying doesn't work on me."

Micah kicked his sneakers against the tile floor and wailed.

"This makes me sad. I wanted you to come to music today."
Andrew turned. "Oh well. Maybe next time."

Victoria started down the hallway. He wasn't going to leave
the child there alone. Was he insane? If the parents found out,
it might open them up for a lawsuit.

He glanced her way, lifted his fingers slightly in a stopping
motion, and shook his head.

She halted.

Reluctantly.

Andrew pointed at the classroom door. "It's a shame,
Micah. We're about to play the rhythm sticks. Those are your
favorite. When you stop crying, you can join us." He walked
into the classroom, making sure to prop the door open.

The boy raised his head. Victoria stepped behind a cabinet
before he spotted her. She waited a few seconds and
peeked out.

Micah's tears dried in an instant as he hopped up. "Hey!
Wait for me."

The child zipped into the classroom. Andrew stuck his
head out. His gaze met hers. He wiggled his eyebrows and
closed the door behind him.

Would the crier really be placated by a pair of sticks? She
had work to do, but curiosity got the better of her. Victoria
walked to the music classroom's door and peered in the
window. Inside, students sat on a large rug with colorful
squares printed on it. Each child stayed in their own square
with a red stick in one hand and a blue stick in the other.

Andrew's back faced her. He typed something on the
computer keyboard at his desk, and classical music filled the
room. She recognized the muted strains of Haydn's Surprise
Symphony through the window.

The children tapped their sticks to the beat as the quiet,
genteel music puttered along. One girl concentrated on her

sticks like she was auditioning for the New York Philharmonic. Tap. Tap. Tap. She played the gentle rhythm.

A loud chord blasted. Victoria jumped.

The children held their sticks in the air and yelled, "Surprise!"

She held her palm over her mouth and chuckled. Even though she was familiar with the notorious loud part of this famous music, it had caught her unaware. Some believed the composer created the unexpected crashing music to wake up sleepers in the audience. It certainly gave *her* heart a jolt. Haydn's practical joke still worked centuries later.

In the classroom, Andrew walked around the students. He appeared taller among the tiny bodies. His shoulders seemed wider too. Did he work out?

Victoria resisted slapping her own forehead. That was no way to be thinking about an employee. She'd been through enough mandatory training classes at the university to realize there was a thin, almost non-existent line between flirting and harassment.

The music teacher could moonlight as a male model. She'd have to be blind not to notice. He was also kind, caring, generous, talented—

Victoria deserved a second slap. Time to return to her office, before he discovered her spying.

She felt a tickle in her nose. Her nostrils twitched. She tried to suppress it.

Ahchoo!

Her body lurched forward. Her head banged the glass. When she looked up, the students and their teacher stared at the window in the door. Andrew made a flourishing gesture at the classroom as if to invite her in.

Victoria waved and retreated.

How humiliating.

She'd been so busy ogling Andrew, she'd disregarded the start of a runny nose. Was she getting sick? Victoria went in search of a tissue.

At her office stood Ronnie and a woman in her late twenties. The bright pink headscarf alerted Victoria to the visitor's identity. The power trip lady from the car line. Sophie's mother.

"Excuse me, Principal Park." Ronnie bit her lip. "I apologize for the interruption, but Mrs. Harris is the mother of one of our kindergartners. She insisted—"

"I want to talk to you." The woman shoved in front of the secretary.

"Do you have an appointment?" Another tickle attacked Victoria's nose. She sniffled, trying not to sneeze in the parent's face.

The muscles under the mother's eyes twitched. "If I had the luxury of making an appointment, I wouldn't be standing here. This is the only free time I have. I'm wasting my lunch hour talking to you."

Victoria sensed an embarrassing scene in the making. She didn't want the entire school subjected to a noisier fit than the one Micah had thrown. Better to take the parent somewhere private.

"Please come in my office, and we can discuss it." She ushered Mrs. Harris inside, making sure the door closed behind them. Victoria pointed at two chairs in front of the desk. "Have a seat. Tell me what's bothering you."

"Your new late fees are what's bothering me." The woman ignored the invitation and invaded her personal space. "My life is hard enough without you draining my bank account of the few pennies I have left. Is this the school's idea of a new fundraiser?"

Victoria stood her ground, refusing to back up. "This isn't

about the money. The teachers are spending their own personal time watching your children after dismissal ends. The students must be picked up by a certain time. It's the rules."

"Rules?" Mrs. Harris scoffed. "Where were these rules for the first half of the school year? I've been picking up my daughter at the same time for months."

"Then her teacher has been working overtime with no extra pay for months. The rules about late pickup weren't enforced, but they were always there. You can check the school handbook."

"Like I've got time!" She jerked away and paced around the small office. "I work all day, pick up Sophie from school, feed her, then spend hours at the nursing home." She stopped in front of Victoria. "My life used to be normal." The pitch of her voice dropped and grew thick with emotion. "I was never late for anything. I had time on the weekends to spend with my daughter. But one bad operation left my mom bedridden."

Victoria tensed. Her vision contracted. Long-suppressed memories flooded. A hospital room. Her precious mother suffering. Ryan railing at the doctor. An instant knot swelled in her throat. The woman's story hit too close to home. The waterworks rushed to her eyes, and she blinked.

"Excuse me." She turned. "I must be coming down with a cold." Victoria grabbed a tissue and made a surreptitious swipe at her nose. Not fully in control, she faced Mrs. Harris. "I'm sorry about your mother's health," she squeezed out between clenched teeth. "I'm sure it must be hard."

"Hard?" Mrs. Harris laughed in an anything-but-humorous tone. "My divorce was hard. Raising my daughter alone is hard. But I always had my momma to back me up. Until now." She lowered her head and took a deep, wavery breath. "Is the world testing how much I can handle? I can't take one more burden. Even something as simple as a two-dollar late fee."

Victoria swallowed. She motioned to the two chairs in front of her desk. "Please. Let's sit." After they were settled, her voice returned to normal. "I'm sorry about your situation. Truly. It must be a constant weight on your shoulders."

Sophie's mom whimpered, head bowed.

Victoria reached out, hesitated, and put her hand over the woman's. "I can't make exceptions for the late policy. It wouldn't be fair to the teachers or the other parents who have to pay."

Mrs. Harris withdrew and swatted the tears from her eyes. "Figures."

"But how about a compromise? What if you leave your daughter for after-school tutoring … with me?"

Mrs. Harris finally looked at her. "What kind of tutoring?"

"Whatever she needs." Victoria smiled. "I used to be a college professor. Kindergarten curriculum is a breeze. I'll wait outside with Sophie and"—she made air quotes with her fingers—"*tutor* your daughter until you pick her up."

"You'd do that?" Mrs. Harris's jaw hung slack.

"As long as you promise not to take advantage of the offer. I don't plan to stay until eight o'clock at night."

"Oh, no." She waved both hands. "It shouldn't be more than fifteen minutes tops. I promise, I just"—she stared—"I can't believe someone like you would help me out."

"Why? Because I'm an old grouch?" Victoria laughed. "Don't trust the gossip. I'm not so bad once you get to know me." She cleared her throat. "And I had a wonderful mother I lost too soon. You should be able to enjoy the time you still have with yours, without having to worry about Sophie."

"Th-thank you." Mrs. Harris launched forward and wrapped Victoria in a tight, weepy hug. "Thank you."

Victoria remained rigid in her hold, uncomfortable at the display of emotion, but not because it was unpleasant.

Awkward, to be sure. But that wasn't the biggest problem. The woman's gratitude made it harder to contain her own tears. For once, someone in Sweetheart was happy with her. She managed to raise a hand and gently pat Mrs. Harris's back.

If Victoria's mother were still here, she'd have been proud of her.

Chapter Twelve

A group of teachers huddled in the break room as Andrew came in search of his second cup of coffee. He waved his Beethoven Rocks mug at them, but they didn't notice. The frantic pitch of their whispers meant something was afoot. He sneaked into the circle as they fumed.

The grandmotherly Mrs. Juarez wrung her hands. Her short, gray curls vibrated. "Have you heard what the old crow is up to now?"

"Who?" Andrew asked.

"Ms. Park." Belinda, the art teacher, slid beside him. "She's the old crow. Always screeching. Peck-peck-pecking away at our peace of mind."

Mrs. Juarez nodded. "Do you know what she's done to our sweet little Sophie? She's making her stay after school every day for tutoring."

"What?" Andrew said. "Why?"

Belinda smirked. "I bet it's because her mother made a scene this morning. The crow's letting Mrs. Harris know who's boss."

Sophie's teacher, Mrs. Dole, crinkled her brow. "It's not

right. The child's behind in reading but not bad. I can catch her up before the end of the year."

Heads shook, and tongues clicked. They might have continued if Victoria hadn't chosen that particular moment to walk into the break room. Conversation ceased.

"Ca-caw," one teacher gave a shrill whisper.

The others giggled. Victoria eyed them over her shoulder, and they froze. Bodies scattered out various exits.

Andrew, mug in hand, stood by the fridge as she chose a paper cup from the stack. She grabbed the carafe of uninspiring brew from the coffee machine. He waited for her to fill her cup, but it appeared she didn't plan to acknowledge him.

"Is it true you're making Sophie Harris stay after school for tutoring?"

Her frame tensed. She lifted the coffee to her lips and took a drink before answering. "Correct."

"Are you sure this is a wise idea?" He stepped closer. "It's admirable you want to help her, but the students spend long enough in school. Sophie needs time to relax and be a kid."

Victoria observed him in silence. Her index finger tapped the cup. "And why is this the music teacher's concern?"

An angry retort jumped to his tongue. Andrew stopped himself and took a breath. "Teachers aren't supposed to show preference, but sometimes you can't help yourself. Sophie is everyone's favorite. Sweet. Loving. A hard worker. I'm sure she can improve her grades during the school day instead of staying late."

"I've discussed the decision with her mother, and Mrs. Harris has agreed." Victoria turned to leave.

"The teachers won't understand this. They'll—"

She rounded. "The teachers' disapproval will not make the slightest difference. And I'd appreciate a modicum of faith in my decisions from all of you. They are made with the school's best interests in mind." She chucked the rest of her drink in the trash. "Can't I get a decent cup of coffee around here?"

Andrew slammed his mug on the counter. Why bother trying to teach her a softer approach? She obviously ignored everything he said. If this continued, the remainder of the school year would be unbearable. How could they survive a dictator like Victoria Park?

SUNLIGHT WARMED THE TOP OF HER HEAD AS VICTORIA SAT ON A bench outside the school. The temperature had risen considerably since morning. She shed her suit jacket and glanced at Sophie beside her. The girl hadn't said a word since Victoria had picked her up from her teacher, Mrs. Dole, at the end of dismissal.

Staff filed by on the way to their cars. Some ignored her. Others gave a blatant stink eye. Andrew must be right. They opposed her tutoring plan, and their displeasure radiated like sound waves from a heavy metal guitar.

She greeted the second-grade teacher who always had crumbs on his shirt. "Goodbye, Mr. Beazley."

He started and gave an awkward cross between a wave and a swat of his hand as he headed for the parking lot.

She waggled her head in mock offense. If they thought the silent treatment would chasten her, they didn't know her very well. She'd inherited her mother's stubborn Italian temperament. Resistance only made her dig in her heels. Perhaps Victoria would take a page from Andrew's book and call out, *Goodbye, sweetie.*

As if on cue, the good-looking music teacher exited the

building. Instead of avoiding her, he walked straight over. A slight afternoon breeze played with his brown hair.

"Hi, Mr. Z." Sophie hopped from the bench and gave him a hug.

"Hey, Sophie." He tapped her nose. "I hope you get to go home soon."

Andrew looked Victoria straight in the eye but said nothing. He turned and walked away.

His snub stung worse than the rest. The whole school was determined to shame her. It was human nature to gossip, but why did everyone hate her to such a ridiculous extent? Was this because she was an outsider?

Sophie returned to her seat and kicked her feet.

Victoria watched the tattered sneakers swing back and forth. What did one talk about with a kindergartner? She searched her brain to remember what she'd enjoyed at that age but came up blank. Had she ever been five years old? Wasn't she born with a diploma in hand?

Victoria cleared her throat. "Is Mr. Zimmerman's class fun?"

Sophie smiled and nodded.

"Did you go to music today?"

She shook her head.

Victoria paused. Maybe she should ask a question that couldn't be answered with a *yes* or *no*. "Where did you go for enrichment?"

"The library." Sophie's voice matched her personality, soft and friendly.

"Do you like to read?"

She nodded.

Oops. Another *yes* or *no* question. Victoria would recalibrate. "Which books are your favorites?"

Sophie scrunched her nose while she thought. "The blue ones."

Victoria blinked. Blue ones? What did that mean?

The sight of Sophie's mom driving into the parking lot saved Victoria from asking. The two of them stood, and the child hopped on one foot.

Mrs. Harris opened the passenger door from inside and leaned toward Victoria, her requisite pink scarf slightly askew. "Thank you, Ms. Park. I owe you one."

Victoria waved. "Don't mention it. See you tomorrow, Sophie."

She grabbed her purse and jacket. She had about half an hour to kill before she was supposed to be at Ryan's house for dinner. Spending the evening with two newlyweds—could her life get any more pathetic?

Victoria needed something to brace herself for the saccharine experience. A double shot espresso, no sugar. Where was the store Andrew Zimmerman bought coffee? She checked her phone for the picture she'd taken of the cup's label.

Heavenly Roasters.

She hoped the place lived up to its name. After searching on the internet for its address, she drove the short three minutes to get there. It operated on a side street off the main drag. Cheerful green-and-white-striped awnings stretched over the windows. Black wrought iron tables sat out front.

She practically ran inside and ordered. A middle-aged woman with a streak of hot pink in her dark, asymmetrical pixie cut rang her up.

Victoria withdrew her wallet but froze when a sign by the register caught her eye. "You don't take credit cards?"

"No. We never got around to buying a machine. Sorry."

"But—" Victoria stared at the woman. Did they also draw their water from a well? "But—" The words refused to form.

But this is the twenty-first century, her brain retorted.

Although true, it wouldn't be kind to say that to the cashier's face.

The woman stuck a hand in the pocket of her apron. "Do you realize the percentage those companies charge small businesses when a customer uses a credit card? It adds up."

"I see." Victoria put her wallet away. "The truth is, I didn't bring any cash. I'm sorry. Perhaps I can stop in later."

The woman squinted and gave her the once-over. "Would you happen to be the new principal at the elementary school? My daughter works there. I've been wanting to meet you."

Oh boy. Another unhappy family member. Victoria braced herself for a fresh onslaught of complaints. What would it be this time? The car line renovations? Forcing the teachers to follow the dress code? Taping off the playground slide until it met safety guidelines?

"I'm Matilda Kelly." The barista smiled. "Amy adores you. She thinks you're the coolest thing since peanut butter and jelly, with your high heels and fancy suits. I imagine she'd try to copy your style if she didn't work with pre-K."

Victoria released the breath she'd been holding. God bless Ms. Amy. At least one person in Sweetheart was on her side.

"I tell you what." Mrs. Kelly slapped the counter. "This espresso is on the house. It'll earn me Brownie points with my baby girl." She scooped the coffee into a metal holder and slid it into the machine. A delicious whirring sounded. The aroma of freshly ground beans filled the air.

"Oh, I couldn't accept," Victoria said, even as she leaned over the counter, staring at the espresso-in-progress with all the subtlety of a puppy eyeing a treat.

The proprietor waved. "Consider it my welcome-to-town present. If it tastes good, come back with cash next time."

"I assure you"—Victoria clasped her hands under her chin—"I will be your most devoted regular."

"Sorry." Mrs. Kelly flipped the switch and poured the coffee into a tan paper cup. "The position's already filled. Andrew Zimmerman comes in here every morning like he's bought stock in the place. I ought to name a daily special after him."

Somehow the declaration irked Victoria. The whole town loved Mr. Z. She couldn't get away from him.

She kept smiling anyway. "He's the reason I found your place. After Mr. Zimmerman brought me one of your scrumptious concoctions, I made it my mission to find you."

Mrs. Kelly passed the cup to Victoria's eager hands.

She took a long draught and sighed. "You're an angel of mercy. Thanks to you, I can brave the trial awaiting me."

Dinner with her brother might have been a pleasant prospect if it didn't include his new wife. Was there an opposite of a thank-you note? If so, she should buy one for Katherine. Because of her, Victoria was stuck in a backwater town, whose citizens detested her.

Her pushy sister-in-law roped her into the worst job of her life on the day after they met. Now that they knew each other better, who knew what Katherine might attempt?

Victoria took another swig to brace herself. "Many thanks for the coffee, Mrs. Kelly. I'll see you tomorrow."

The barista laughed. "Don't mention it."

The bell jingled on the front door, and Andrew Zimmerman walked into the store. At the sight of Victoria, his shoulder jerked to the left as if he might bolt. He paused and gave her a polite smile.

It in no way resembled the normal sunny expression he'd greeted her with in the past.

Another friend lost. What was it about her that drove people away? Victoria allowed herself a two-second pity party before shaking it off. This was better. More professional. Maybe he'd leave her alone and stop trying to apply psychological sandpaper to her personality.

"Mr. Zimmerman." Victoria's chin dipped once as she passed. She drank her coffee with one hand and opened the door with her other.

No more empathy lessons. No more surprise meatloaf deliveries. And no more making it hard to ignore the under-the-surface attraction sizzling between them.

Andrew considered hightailing it when he spotted Victoria.

Correction.

Not Victoria. Ms. Park. She wanted things professional, so he'd think of her that way. But no matter how much he wished to avoid *Ms. Park*, his taste buds craved one of Mrs. Kelly's caramel macchiatos.

His taciturn boss made it easy by leaving first, and the tight line between his shoulder blades relaxed. He couldn't avoid her forever, but he'd engage as little as possible. Her methods had soured his desire to build any kind of relationship.

The doorbell alerted him of her exit. He studied the frustrating woman through the store window. The late afternoon sunlight glinted off her black hair like silk.

Silk?

He shook his head. Like a crow's wing. An angry, squawking crow.

Andrew walked to the counter and winked at Mrs. Kelly. "Did you miss me?"

"I was about to burst into tears." She got to work making

his drink, not bothering to wait for an order. "I understand I have you to thank for my new customer." She squeezed caramel syrup into the cup, swirled it around, and moved to the machine.

Andrew's nostrils expanded as the scent of steamed milk wafted. "Who?"

"Ms. Park. She said you brought her one of my drinks. I'm glad I got the chance to meet her."

Something between a groan and a huff left Andrew's lips. "You may be the only person in town who feels that way."

The machine drip-drip-dripped the rich, brown liquid into a mug. Mrs. Kelly mixed the nectar together and drizzled golden syrup along the foamy top. "I know for a fact I'm not. Amy just adores her." She set the finished masterpiece in front of him.

"Is that so?" Andrew took the white, porcelain mug.

She crossed her arms. "My baby girl inherited her daddy's shy disposition. Can't speak up to save her life. From what I hear, she almost dissolved into the pavement when a mother chewed her out in the car line. Until Ms. Park dashed in and took over. Amy's gushed about it more than once."

Andrew raised the fresh macchiato to his lips. The warm liquid saturated his taste buds in a calming swell. He wouldn't spoil Ms. Kelly's good opinion. Principal Park might have rescued the timid Ms. Amy from an angry parent, but she was also the one who orchestrated the car line confrontation. How much credit did she deserve for fixing a problem she'd created?

Chapter Thirteen

Victoria collapsed on her brother's couch. "My feet hate me even more than the teachers do. I should buy a pedometer to track how many steps I'm walking."

"Now I know what to get you for your birthday." Ryan sat across from her on the cushy, gray armchair as his two Yorkies cavorted around the living room. "Apart from your aching appendages, what do you think of the elementary setting? Have you found your calling?"

She kicked off her patent leather heels and propped her feet on the cushions. "Yeah right. I never thought I'd miss reading dissertation papers, but nothing is worse than pre-K."

An oven door slammed. Katherine called from the kitchen, "Dinner's almost ready. I'm sorry it's a little burnt around the edges!"

Her brother chuckled. The puppy with the pink bow pawed at his ankle, and Ryan lifted her to his lap. "Consider it good training. After this experience, working with college students and professors will be a breeze. It's an administrative boot camp."

"And my troops are ready to revolt. Why does everyone

despise me?" Victoria flopped over and laid her head on the couch's arm. "They're calling me the old crow."

Ryan snort laughed but stopped when she glared at him.

She pointed. "If I hear one more *ca-caw* outside my office door, I'll scream. All I've done since I arrived at Sweetheart Elementary is strive to make things better. Yet the staff resents me for it."

With protruding lips, her brother considered her. "You remind me of someone else who's always on a crusade to improve things."

"Who?"

The clang of a dropped metal pan rang from the kitchen. Romeo raced to investigate the sound. Ryan thumbed a finger in that direction and grinned.

Victoria bristled. "I don't appreciate being compared to your wife. I'm sure she has many lovely characteristics, but you have to admit, she's the female incarnation of a bulldozer."

Instead of getting offended, Ryan laughed.

She sighed and returned to the subject at hand. "Why do all the teachers refuse to let me help?"

A particular teacher with honey-colored hair and sparkling brown eyes popped into her mind. Except they didn't sparkle anymore. At least not at her.

"Wait a minute." Ryan raised a hand. "Are you *helping*"— he made air quotes—"like you used to help in high school? When you bossed your best friend around and told her she should break up with her boyfriend?"

"Someone had to point out the guy was a loser. He cheated on her three times."

"But when you revealed such painful, albeit true, information, did it change anything?"

She remained silent.

He chucked a throw pillow at her. "Did it?"

"No!" Victoria sat up and tossed it back at his head. "I'll never understand why she kept dating him. The jerk. But I fail to see your point."

"If you'd approached your best friend with sympathy instead of sarcasm, she might have listened. I imagine the same thing goes for the school staff. Be less hard-nosed, and maybe they'll take a minute to consider your perspective. It's all in the delivery. Don't just command. Show them your heart."

She glared at him. "I can understand why you became a political consultant. You're great at schmoozing."

"Yes, he is." Katherine walked into the living room wearing a sauce-splattered apron. "It was definitely *not* the reason I fell in love with him."

Ryan moved the puppy to the side of the armchair, pulled his wife on his lap, and kissed a red smear on her cheek. "Let me guess. We're having spaghetti."

"Bingo." She wrapped an arm around him.

Victoria shuddered. The childish urge to pretend she was throwing up assailed her. Another sign the elementary environment was a bad influence. What came next? Telling knock-knock jokes? She had to get out of this town. They'd find another interim principal. If she climbed in her borrowed sedan and kept driving until she reached New York, her brother could box her stuff and mail it later.

Ryan interrupted her mental escape plan. "How goes it with Andrew?"

She trained her eyes on the carpet. "What do you mean?"

"You two seemed to be hitting it off at the wedding. Doesn't interacting with him every workday give you ideas?"

"On the contrary"—Victoria lowered her feet to the floor and adjusted her pinstripe, knee-length skirt—"he's one of the many people who can't stand me."

"What!" Katherine unwound her arm from Ryan's neck. "I thought he was smart enough to appreciate an intelligent woman. How disappointing."

"Don't blame him too much." For some ridiculous reason, Victoria felt obligated to defend the charismatic music teacher. "He's been helpful on more than one occasion. But we had a ... a disagreement over a student. He misunderstood my motives, and I'm not at liberty to divulge the whole story."

Her brother quirked his eyebrows. "I hate to harp on the same string, but my earlier advice applies in this situation as well. Even if you can't reveal the details, show Andrew your heart. He might give you the benefit of the doubt." Ryan nudged Katherine onto her feet and stood. "I'm starving. Let's eat."

The newlyweds canoodled their way to the kitchen, leaving Victoria alone with her jumbled thoughts.

It was easy for her happily married little brother to dole out relationship advice. That didn't make it easy to follow. There were many reasons she couldn't show Andrew her heart.

Number one, he didn't care to see it.

Number two, she was his boss.

And the third and most important reason her heart must remain a mystery was that she hadn't used the neglected thing in so long, there must be rust in her emotional arteries.

Chapter Fourteen

Perspiration on Victoria's forehead belied the nippy winter weather. She opened the dusty pickup door with smile firmly fixed. The driver would never guess her temples were pounding like a pair of Andrew's rhythm sticks. If she could make it through the car line, she'd get an aspirin from her purse.

"Good morning." Her stuffy nose muffled her greeting.

She hurried to the next car, swung the door wide, and repeated the salutation. Victoria surveyed the line and released a sound halfway between a sigh and a groan. She'd opened three doors while the aide behind her worked on the first one.

How long had it been since she first instituted her new procedure? The four-page handout was very clear. And she'd given a refresher in the last staff meeting. Did she have to explain again?

Open. Greet. Move on.

It wasn't rocket science!

She scrutinized the winding parade of cars. Andrew was at the end, servicing vehicles and ushering kids at a rate that put even her impressive total to shame. Of course, it helped when the kids leapt from the cars in a rush to hug their favorite teacher. But still. If he weren't her employee, she'd be tempted to swoon at his car line prowess.

Victoria checked the time. Three minutes until the cut-off, and parents were backed out on the street. She picked up her pace. There were two more cars between the next teacher and her. If she emptied them, they could wave the whole line through and get the last stretch of cars into the parking lot. She finished a red coupe and raced past the oak tree to the next vehicle.

Clang!

Pain knifed through her right foot. She stumbled to the side and looked down. Her pointy-toed flat stuck in the bent iron teeth of the water drainage grate.

"Gah!" She gasped, jerked her foot from the trapped shoe, and tried to move her toes.

Ms. Amy ran up and placed a hand on her back. "Are you okay, Ms. Park?"

Victoria concentrated on breathing. She yanked her flat from the grate, slipped her foot into the shoe, and waved the woman away. "Fine," she gritted out between clenched teeth. "Please finish the cars."

Ms. Amy's hands fluttered in the direction of the injured foot, but she balled them into fists, pressed them to her chest, and obeyed.

Victoria limped to her original spot while the empty cars passed. A new row pulled in front of her. She hobbled to each vehicle and managed to get the doors open despite the pain. The line departed, she glanced at her watch, and whooped.

"Seven fifty-one. We did it!" She'd jump for joy if her right big toe didn't feel like it was pierced by a red-hot needle.

The teachers and aides passed her on their way to class. She waited until they disappeared before attempting to walk.

The first step was painful. The second was worse. She inched to the curb and sat. Once she removed her shoe, the ugly purple truth stared back.

A voice behind her spoke. "Why is your foot the color of a mulberry?"

Andrew hovered over her. Victoria tried to put on her shoe, but the swelling made it impossible. He crouched and examined the bruise.

"Does this hurt?" He placed a gentle finger on top of her big toe.

"Agh!" She swatted him away. "Yes!"

"Can you move it?"

Victoria tried to wiggle her toe, but it didn't receive the message. She concentrated all her energy on the uncooperative appendage, willing it to bend the tiniest centimeter.

It didn't budge.

Andrew eyed her. "Pretty sure you broke it."

"What? I slammed it on the grate. It must be numb. That's all."

"Uh-huh." He stood and offered her a hand. "Then you can walk to your office?"

Victoria accepted the assistance and wobbled to her feet. "Absolutely." She gripped her shoe, tried to take another step on her bare foot, and winced.

Andrew rubbed a hand over his eyes. "I know you won't relish this, but write me a demerit later." He scooped her into his arms.

She squealed. "Are you crazy? What if the parents see?"

He strode across the pavement without responding.

"Mr. Zimmerman, put me down." She squirmed. "Now!"

His gaze cut to her. "Principal Park, I'm saving you a twenty-minute hobble to your office. This might look great in the movies, but the truth is, you're kind of heavy. Please cut me some slack."

Victoria clamped her tongue between her teeth. He was right—as much as she hated to admit it. She couldn't make it inside by herself, and she loathed making a scene almost as much as being told she was heavy.

"Let's find a compromise," she ground out. "Please deposit me on the bench by the front door and go find a rolling chair. It will be much less incendiary if you wheel me to the office."

A disgusted snort issued from his nostrils.

Victoria glared at him. Embarrassment, anger, and something else she'd rather not define warred inside of her. She tried to ignore the muscles shifting beneath her legs, the rock-hard chest pressed against her.

Was he always this warm? His body radiated heat on the chilly January morning, toasting her insides like a marshmallow. Her objections melted on the spot.

Andrew approached the entrance, set her gently on the bench, and went inside the school. Victoria placed a hand to her cheek. It burned to the touch. Was her face the color of a sun-ripened tomato?

She waited for a good ten minutes. If he was so quick to open car doors, how long did it take to fetch something to transport her to the office?

Finally, Ronnie rushed from the building, pushing a wheeled desk chair. "Oh, sugar, are you hurt bad?" She bent to examine the bruise. "Whoo-ee! You smacked it good, didn't you?"

Victoria waved to where Andrew had disappeared. "Did Mr. Zimmerman—"

"It was time for music class. He sent me instead. I'll roll you to your office."

"Oh"—she rose and slid onto the chair—"good for him. I appreciate his dependable attitude. Punctuality is a virtue."

An overrated virtue. Compared to helping a fellow human in desperate need.

Victoria fumed as the secretary carted her through the glass double doors. She didn't appreciate being abandoned without a by-your-leave, but logic reasserted itself. This was easier. It gave her the opportunity to recover before she had to approach the attractive music teacher again. After being princess-carried across the parking lot, it was difficult to maintain professional boundaries.

ANDREW MUNCHED ON THE UNINSPIRING BURRITO HE'D NUKED IN THE break room's microwave. It needed another minute. The lukewarm taste left much to be desired, but he was too distracted to care.

Was Principal Park okay?

It galled him to leave her when she was injured. But Ronnie was more than trustworthy. The competent secretary must have made sure their boss found a ride to the doctor.

"Hello, Andrew." Belinda sashayed into the room. The colors on her skirt swirled like an impressionist painting.

"Hey, Belinda." He managed to choke down another bite of burrito. It was colder than the first.

"I hear I missed quite the scene when you played the movie hero and carried Ms. Park."

His eyes rolled up as he took a third bite.

"Sorry you suffered through that." She patted his arm. "If only it had been me instead. Some girls get all the breaks." She giggled. "Get it? Breaks?"

Andrew swallowed. "What happened to Ms. Park?"

"Last I saw, she was in her office."

"What? She didn't go get her foot checked out?"

"I guess. Must not have been serious—"

Andrew chucked the rest of his lunch into the trash can and stormed from the break room. He stopped at the principal's office, but she wasn't there. Perhaps Belinda was mistaken.

He wandered to the front counter, where Ronnie was finishing a call.

"Hello, my lovely." He tapped her desk. "I was wondering how Ms. Park is doing. What did the doctor say?"

"Nothing." Her lips wrinkled. "Since the doctor didn't see her. I spent ten minutes trying to convince that woman to leave. The most I could do was make her sit in her office with her foot propped up and tucked under an ice pack."

Andrew sighed. "She couldn't even manage that much. Her office is empty."

"The most difficult principal I ever met." Ronnie clicked her tongue. "Hardworking as all get out. No doubt, she's somewhere around here fixing something. But I wish she'd find an easier way of going about it."

He ruffled his hair. "Maybe the injury will slow her down."

"Pffft. You don't believe that any more than I do."

"Why don't you go find her?"

"And say what?" She leaned back. "Threaten her with detention if she doesn't stay put? I'm no fool. I recognize a lost cause when I see one." Ronnie looked him over. "Now, if you were to ask, it might be a different story."

"What do you mean?"

"Ms. Park plows through any arguments with all the finesse of a battering ram, but at least she listens to yours first. The rest of us don't get the time of day. With you, it's special." Her eyes twinkled. "I have my own suspicions about why."

A few weeks ago, her insinuations would have pleased him.

But that was before he decided to cut out any personal interactions with Victoria and treat her solely as his superior. He checked his watch. He had fifteen minutes of lunch break before a class came. Might as well make sure his superior was doing all right.

For the school's sake.

"Excuse me, Ronnie. I'll see if I can track her down. Are you willing to drive Ms. Park to the doctor if I convince her to leave?"

"How are you going to accomplish such a feat?" She smirked. "Carry her to the car?"

He winked. "You'll have to wait and see."

Chapter Fifteen

Step. Pain. Step. Pain.

Victoria shuffled along the sidewalk, ignoring the complaints her foot telegraphed. She had a meeting with the procrastinating maintenance man about the dangerous grate and intended to use her injury as Exhibit A.

Passing the playground, she spotted a class at recess and Sophie picking wildflowers from the grass. The main reason Victoria hadn't left the campus was that little girl. Mrs. Harris depended on the deal they'd made. Victoria couldn't let her down. She'd visit the emergency room after the school day ended.

Sophie noticed her and ran over, tiny white blossoms in hand. She kept pace with Victoria as she limped. The thin, pensive face stared up at her.

Victoria stopped. "Hello, Sophie. Is there something you wanted?"

Her miniature stalker spoke. "I want to give you a hug."

Another hug? Victoria would never grow used to the endless flow of embraces from tiny strangers whose names she couldn't remember. Of course, this was the one name she knew.

Sophie raised a hand and pulled it back. "*Can* I give you a hug?"

Victoria studied her. She wore jeans and an oversized T-shirt, frayed at the collar. Her black hair stuck out from her head in a springy riot. Uncertainty shone from dark, questioning eyes.

It was the first time one of the children had asked. Normally, they launched themselves at her like she was a fairy-tale princess at an amusement park.

"Yes, Sophie. You can hug me."

She walked closer, wrapped her arms around Victoria's legs, and squeezed. Victoria gave the girl an awkward pat. The shirt felt slightly damp. Sophie released her and ran off.

"What do you think you're doing?" a frustrated male voice called.

She started and looked over her shoulder.

Andrew Zimmerman stormed her way with a scowl.

Victoria's cheeks reddened. "I was just giving her a hug. She asked for it."

"I don't mean Sophie." He pointed at her shoe, where the discolored flesh puffed above the leather seam. "I mean you walking around campus on a broken foot."

"We don't know it's broken." She rotated her ankle. "It might be sprained. I hit it pretty hard. The swelling's diminished—"

"Why risk it? The emergency room is a ten-minute drive from here. Let Ronnie take you. If I'm wrong, you can return with plenty of time to wreak havoc on the school."

Havoc? That's how he viewed her efforts. The description pricked her heart, but she didn't show it.

Victoria leveled a cold glare at him. "I have something

important to do, which can't be put off. I'll visit the doctor afterward."

"What's so important?"

"It's none of your business." She tried to stomp away.

Bad idea. Her body lurched. The throbbing in her right foot intensified.

"Gah!" She wobbled and slumped to a sitting position on the ground.

Andrew crouched at her side. He placed a gentle hand on the toe of her shoe. His head drifted near her own. A subtle, woodsy scent enveloped her. His cologne. Her eyes shut as she inhaled. It took her back to the first time they met.

Slow dancing at Ryan's wedding. Andrew's tall, firm body pressed against hers. The all too brief taste of his lips.

Was that the last time she'd felt happy? Probably. Not that Andrew's presence was the reason. Okay. It was part of the reason. But also because she'd expected to hear about her promotion to associate dean at any moment.

Success had been within reach. Only to be ripped away.

"I can't leave you on the ground." Andrew's voice broke her reverie. "Do you want me to carry you?"

Her eyelids flew open. She scooted backward. "Is that a threat?"

His brows dipped. "Of course not. Did it sound like one?"

His offer to carry her was a definite threat—to her peace of mind.

Victoria placed her palms against the cool pavement. She scrambled up, leaning on her left foot to help mitigate the pain. "Thank you for your offer of assistance, but I'll walk." She faltered a half step as if to prove it.

He straightened. "It's stupid to put yourself through the pain. If you don't prefer to be carried, let me get the chair and roll you inside."

"No, thank you." Victoria managed another stuttery step. "You must have a class to teach. I'll take care of myself and head for the doctor after work."

Andrew crowded into her space, the difference in their heights more noticeable when she wasn't wearing heels. The way her foot throbbed, she wondered if she'd ever wear stilettos again. She moved, and a half whimper escaped.

His eyes narrowed. "What could possibly be important enough to put yourself through this torture?"

Maybe his proximity short-circuited her brain, because she answered with the truth. "Sophie's tutoring. I told her mother—"

"That's it?" A look of disgust crossed Andrew's face. "You'd risk your health just to stick it to Sophie's mom? How big is your ego?"

She double blinked. "It's not about ego. Sophie's mother needs ... I promised to ... Forget it."

Victoria gave the slow-motion version of spinning on her heel and stalking away. It was more like careening to the side and step-hopping toward the building, but at least it put some distance between her and the man who drove her crazy.

Let him think what he chose. A few more months, and she'd be free of this provincial place forever. If her brother ever wanted to spend the holidays together, he'd have to come to her in New York.

Chapter Sixteen

Victoria drove down Main Street as Pachelbel's Canon in D played through her radio. The gentle, well-ordered music calmed her disquieted soul. It helped that the weekend stretched ahead of her with a peaceful promise.

For once, she'd left school before the sun set. After five days of unending pushback from the staff and her recent stop at the urgent care, she was ready for a little fun. Eating a meal she didn't heat in the microwave was about as wild as this Friday afternoon was going to get. A far cry from her clubbing college days, but it would have to do.

She parked in front of The Brunch Café and hobbled from the car to the front door. Getting anywhere took twice as long with the walking cast on her foot. She'd passed the restaurant often, but this was her first time trying it out.

She paused at the door where a sign was posted in the window. It read, "Credit card machine broken. Cash only."

"Not again." Victoria checked her purse.

She almost did a fist pump when she discovered a twenty-dollar bill in the side pocket. Her stomach reminded her of its empty status with a gurgle. She'd skipped lunch.

Victoria grabbed the door handle and entered. The plastic cast clunked against the black-and-white-checkered floor. Cherry-red booths, linoleum tabletops, and vintage signs on the walls conveyed a retro charm.

It hummed with customers at the close-set tables. She debated whether or not to dine in. Eating alone didn't bother her, but her foot did. The earlier knifing pain had subsided into a fiery throb. Perhaps she'd order takeout, head home, and prop her fractured toe on a pillow.

Hairline fracture, to be exact. But it was enough to make getting around a chore.

She'd never broken more than a fingernail in her entire life. The fact she'd cracked a bone during car line frustrated her. Sweetheart, Texas, should come with a message from the surgeon general. *Warning: This town contains over-opinionated people, toe-eating drainage grates, and very few credit card machines.*

Victoria limped to the Formica counter and sat on a vinyl-topped stool. She slipped a menu from behind the silver napkin dispenser.

A pretty blonde with a name tag identifying her as Susanna approached. "Hello." She pulled a pad and pencil from her apron pocket. "May I take your order?"

"It's my first time. What would you recommend?"

"As the owner, I'd recommend the most expensive dish on the menu." She laughed. "But anything is good."

Remembering her cash budget, Victoria checked the prices. She pondered before ordering the meatloaf. It might not be as good as Andrew's, but she'd been craving another slice.

Susanna left to help a group at a nearby booth, and Victoria swiveled on the stool to observe the diners while she waited.

Her nostrils twitched, and she dug in her purse, searching for a tissue. She found it in time to cover her mouth before a sneeze racked her body.

It wasn't the first. She'd been blowing her nose and sneezing at random times throughout the day. Maybe she was allergic to Sweetheart.

A bell on the front door jingled as a new customer entered. Belinda Carlyle, the art teacher, stood inside the threshold. She glanced over at Victoria with a slight tipping of her nose.

Victoria leaned back on the counter and folded her hands on her lap. She refused to pretend she hadn't noticed the snub. But she also wouldn't respond to bad manners with more of the same.

The bell rang again, and a tall figure almost bumped into Belinda. Andrew Zimmerman tottered to the side. "Whoa." He grabbed Belinda's upper arms to steady them both. "Were you waiting to greet me at the door?"

She giggled and batted her eyelashes faster than a hummingbird's wings. "I was deciding where to sit."

He looked around the diner, and his eyes locked with Victoria's. Andrew gave a curt nod. His attention returned to Belinda. The chatter of diners and the clink of silverware on plates hid their conversation.

Victoria analyzed the pair. The art teacher made her crush obvious on a daily basis, but Andrew treated her with the same friendliness he showed every colleague.

Until now.

The two were standing awfully close. Were they meeting for dinner? Like a date?

She pushed the thought from her mind. It was none of her business either way. All she wanted was food. Another sneeze shook her.

Food and another tissue.

~

Andrew noted the way Belinda's body arched closer to his. He shifted his weight to put a bit of distance between them, but she quickly followed. He scanned the room, his gaze touching on Victoria for the briefest second.

Their eyes met. Held. She turned her back and picked up a menu. She was alone at the counter. He couldn't see her feet from where he stood. Had she even gone to the doctor?

Frustrating woman.

Her ramrod posture betrayed no hint of weariness. Was she a machine? Untouched by pain or human emotion?

"Oh, Andrew. You're just in time to rescue me." Belinda latched on to his arm with the tenacity of a music student who wanted a specific instrument. "I hate dining alone. It feels pathetic. Since we're both here, why don't you eat with me?"

"Well, I—" His glance cut to Victoria.

Correction. Not Victoria. Ms. Park.

"You'd be saving me from a fate worse than death." Belinda's fingers tightened. "It's so mortifying to eat by myself."

Her wide, brown eyes reminded him of a kid standing alone at recess while all the others played with their friends. How could he reject the sincere plea?

Andrew smiled. "Sure."

She gave an enthusiastic bounce and looped her arm around his. "Great. Let's take that booth over there."

Belinda steered him toward the back corner. He passed their principal on the way and glimpsed a black, plastic walking cast on her foot. At least she'd sought medical help.

Susanna Sheppard exited the kitchen and set a paper bag on the counter with a cheery, "One meatloaf to go."

"Thank you." Ms. Park rose from her stool. She slipped a twenty across the counter.

Meatloaf? Andrew wondered if her order was a coincidence. Or was she hankering for more of his cooking?

"Here we are!" Belinda slid into one side of the booth.

Andrew took the seat by the wall, facing out to the restaurant. Belinda sat in front of him. In his peripheral vision, he spotted Ms. Park walking to the exit. The door opened as she reached for it.

Mrs. Harris and Sophie entered.

"Ms. Park!" Sophie's mom beamed.

He couldn't hear what else was said, but Mrs. Harris in no way resembled the angry parent who'd recently stalked through the school halls.

"Hello-oooo." A hand waved in front of his face.

"Huh?" Andrew hadn't realized he was bent to the side, peering around Belinda.

The vinyl booth squeaked as she moved parallel to him. "I'm starved. Aren't you?"

"Uh, yeah." He grabbed a menu from where it rested between the wall and the napkin dispenser. "Let me figure out what I want."

His eyes darted to the pair talking by the door.

Belinda's head bobbed in front of his line of sight. Her lips parted in a cheery smile. "Would you order me a water?" She slipped her purse strap over her shoulder. "I'm going to freshen my makeup. Be right back."

"Okay." With great effort, he kept his gaze trained on her. Belinda slid out of the booth and disappeared through the door leading to the restrooms.

His attention returned to the entrance, but Ms. Park was gone. Sophie and her mom walked through the diner and stopped at a table near his. The little girl beamed when she saw him.

"Hi, Mr. Z!" Sophie bounded to his side and wrapped her arms around him.

"Hello." He laughed.

Her mother joined them with a sigh. "I wish she got that happy to see me. You're definitely her favorite. Although, you're in danger of being replaced."

"What's this?" He scowled in pretend dismay. "Who's trying to steal Sophie away from me?"

Mrs. Harris chuckled. "My daughter can't get enough of Ms. Park. She was downright disappointed when I picked her up from school today."

Andrew tried to hide his surprise. "And you're not upset about the extra tutoring?"

"Tutoring?" Mrs. Harris's brow crinkled. "Oh, right! Tutoring. No, I'm not upset. She's doing me a favor."

"A favor?" He processed the new information. "I thought she forced you to leave Sophie at school late."

"Forced me? No way." A sheepish expression appeared. "The truth is ... Ms. Park called it *tutoring* to save my pride." She looked around before whispering, "I guess it's okay to tell you, Mr. Zimmerman. I couldn't get off work any sooner, but I can't afford the late pick-up fees. The principal offered to stay with Sophie every day until I got there."

Andrew didn't respond.

Couldn't.

Guilt paralyzed his tongue.

Victoria was babysitting Sophie as a favor to the same person who'd railed at her in the hallway? And then she'd kept quiet about it to allow the woman to save face?

Mrs. Harris pressed her lips together and shook her head. "I still can't believe she'd do that for me. I admit, I'd rather my situation not get around"—she took a shuddery breath—"but I don't want you thinking bad of Ms. Park. Her heart's twenty-four karats and then some."

"Whose heart?" Belinda returned to the table. "Hi, Sophie." She grinned at the girl.

Sophie gave a sunny wave.

Andrew cleared his throat. "Mrs. Harris told me our new principal is doing a good job."

"Really?" Belinda wore the pleasant, open-eyed expression teachers used when they were humoring a parent. "So glad to hear it."

Sophie and her mom said goodbye and left for their own table. Belinda slid into the booth, swiveled away from the Harris family, and screwed her lips into a disbelieving pucker. "At least one person likes the old crow." She snickered. "Isn't her nickname a riot?"

Andrew remained silent. Sophie's mother preferred her circumstances not be made public, and he had to respect her feelings. But Victoria carried the blame for a crime she didn't commit.

His emotions whirled as his coworker chattered. Because of a little gossip, he'd leveled unfounded accusations at Victoria. Lectured her when he had no clue what he was talking about.

He'd been a jerk.

No wonder she'd turned her back to him.

Had he torpedoed his chances with her forever?

Chapter Seventeen

ndrew stood outside Victoria's door with a paper bag in hand. He had no idea if she was a sweets person, but he'd brought dessert from the café. Susanna made the best red velvet cake in town.

He knocked. No answer. Her car sat in the driveway. She couldn't have gone to bed at six o'clock. He knocked again.

A muffled voice called from the other side. Several seconds passed before the door opened. Victoria stood in her work clothes—her once crisp Oxford shirt a wrinkled, untucked mess. The hem of her black skirt hiked higher on one side, and her bare toes of the foot not wearing a walking cast curled on the carpeted floor.

The sounds of a string quartet drifted from inside. His fingers twitched in response. Beethoven's No. 14, if he wasn't mistaken.

She stared at him in a daze.

"Good evening." Andrew took in her drowsy countenance. "Did I wake you up?"

"No." She yawned as if to contradict the words. "Can I help you?"

He held up the bag. "I've brought a reward for your hectic week. Susanna's red velvet cake is good for all sorts of ailments. Maybe it will help your toe heal faster."

"I'm more of a pie person"—she stared at the bag for several seconds before continuing—"buuuuuuut it was rude of me to say that to your face. I'm—" Her head jerked back. A violent sneeze exploded. "I'm sorry." Victoria massaged her temples. "I think the painkiller the doctor prescribed for my foot has affected my brain. Thank you for the considerate gesture." She took the bag.

He waited for her to close the door, but she stood unmoving. Her gaze pointed somewhere around his earlobe.

He ducked to make eye contact. "Are you okay?"

"I'm not sure." Her voice rasped, and she cleared her throat. "I've experienced the occasional sneezing and runny nose for a few days. But it's getting worse. Now it hurts to swallow."

"Uh-oh. Looks like they got you."

"What?" She focused on him for the first time since opening the door. "Who?"

"The kids. They're the cutest germ carriers you'll ever meet. My first year of teaching, I took sick leave three times with upper respiratory infections."

"Great." She moaned. "What helped you recover?"

"I tried medicine, vitamins, rancid garlic-honey-lemon home remedies that made me gag." He scrunched his face. "Sorry to tell you this, but the best thing is lots of rest."

"Got it." She started to shut the door. "Thanks for the cake. Good night."

"Wait!" He propped a hand on the doorjamb. "Medicine helps speed up the process. I have some cough syrup in my apartment. I'll get it for you."

Andrew withdrew before she said *yay* or *nay*, retrieved the decongestant from his place, and returned to Victoria's door. She'd left it open. He knocked once and entered. She was lying on the couch, stretched on her back, with a pillow propped under her head, one arm flung over her eyes.

He reviewed the medicine bottle to make sure it was safe to take with the painkiller then gave her shoulder a gentle tap. "Ready for the cough syrup?"

She opened her mouth without a word. He chuckled, poured a large dose into the clear plastic cap, and tipped it to her soft, pink lips. She drank the thick liquid and gagged.

Her fingers balled into fists. "That stuff tastes like cherry-flavored acid."

"Mmm-hmm." Andrew nodded. "Burns the kiddie cooties right out of you."

She cracked her lids open. Serious, dark eyes studied him. Victoria propped her hands on the cushions and scooted to a sitting position. "Is Belinda here too?"

"Who?"

"The art teacher." She wrapped her arms around her body. "You two were having dinner together at the café."

"We weren't having—" He shifted from one foot to another. "I mean, we happened to run into each other. An impromptu thing. With a friend."

"I see."

Andrew rocked on his heels. Should he sit down or wait to be invited? Harmony filled the uncomfortable space between them. The sounds of viola, cello, and double violins floated around them in a gentle collaboration of beauty.

He raised a finger in the air. "Nice music."

Victoria nodded. "It relaxes me. When I have too many worries in my brain, music irons them out."

Neither of them spoke as the instruments wove an intricate web of melody and counterpoint.

Victoria yawned. "I appreciate the cough syrup." She waved at the paper bag on the coffee table. "And the cake. You win my vote for neighbor of the year. But don't waste any more of your weekend on me. I'll take care of myself."

He placed the medicine bottle on the end table by her head. "I'll leave this here. Drink another dose in four hours."

"Mmmm." Her eyes closed. She reclined and turned on her side. "Four hours," she murmured into the pillow. "Got it."

Andrew headed for the door. He hesitated and glanced at Victoria's still form. His brain debated whether or not to leave a sick person to fend for herself. Kind of heartless.

Plus, now might be the optimal time to mend fences—while she was too weak to argue.

RATTLING WOKE VICTORIA FROM A DEEP SLUMBER. SHE LIFTED HER head from the pillow and sat up. Her limbs hung useless, weighed down by exhaustion or a cough syrup hangover. She wasn't sure which.

How long had she been asleep?

Running water sounded from the kitchen. On a normal night, she might call 9-1-1. But her brain felt like oatmeal, and she couldn't work up the energy to be scared.

She hauled herself from the couch and stumbled toward the noise. Stopping in the doorway, she watched as Andrew Zimmerman placed a tea kettle on the stove.

Where had the kettle come from? Her sister-in-law must have left it. Or perhaps Andrew brought it from his apartment. Or ... or ... Thoughts fought to push through the cotton in her head.

Hadn't he gone home?

She remembered his giving her medicine. How long ago?

Victoria glanced at the clock on the wall. 12:00.

Was that a.m. or p.m.?

She wobbled into the room and sank onto a chair at the table.

Andrew slipped a mug from the cabinet and placed it in front of her. "It's midnight, in case you're wondering."

"I was." She wrapped her fingers around the empty cup. "What are you doing here?"

"Figured you could use some tea." He smiled. "Don't worry. No garlic included." He puttered around the room.

Her eyelids drooped. She yawned and shook her head.

Must wake up.

The kettle whistled. Andrew grabbed it from the stove and poured the steaming liquid into her mug. He steeped a tea bag in the water, added honey, and stirred. Motioning with both hands to the drink, he faked a French accent. "Bon appétit."

She raised the concoction to her lips, blew on the tea, and took a tentative sip. It coated the inside of her mouth with tingly goodness. She swallowed. "Nice. Thank you."

He sat across from her. "I hope it wasn't too weird of me to let myself back in. I did knock, but you were out for the count. After you drink the tea, I'll leave you alone."

"You're losing sleep because of me." She drank from the mug. The liquid washed down her aching throat, soothing the scratchy fire.

"I'm a night owl. I'd have been awake anyway." Andrew reached out and stopped just shy of her face. "Have you checked your temperature?"

She squinted at the fingers hovering above her nose. "No. I collapsed on the couch the moment I walked in the door."

He pressed the back of his hand to her forehead. "Do you have a thermometer?"

Victoria's eyes slid shut at his cool touch. "No."

"I'm pretty sure you have a fever. Stay home tomorrow and rest. Lie in bed all day. Without working. Rest."

She opened her eyes. "Why are you repeating yourself?"

His winsome smile appeared. "I imagine it's been years since you spent twenty-four hours doing absolutely nothing. Am I right?" He brushed a strand of hair from her cheek.

What must she look like? Victoria cringed at her wrinkled work outfit. She batted his hand away. "Truth be told, I can't remember the last time I took a day off. But this cold, flu, whatever is a decent excuse. I think I'll take your advice."

"Great decision." Andrew leaned his elbows on the table. His gaze wandered over her face.

Victoria scratched at her eyebrow. Despising the self-conscious gesture, she put both hands around her mug and drank. She finished the tea in three gulps, ignoring how her tongue prickled at the heat, and set the cup on the table with a thunk. "I appreciate your help, but you should go. I can put myself to bed. No need to sing me a lullaby."

He laughed. "That's a relief. For a music teacher, I have a woefully mediocre voice. My singing was the joke of the orchestra."

"Orchestra?"

His gaze dropped, and he stroked the side of his nose. "Yeah. I ... I played in one for a while."

She crossed her arms on the tabletop, mirroring Andrew's position. "Symphony? Jazz? Big band?"

"Symphony." The corner of his mouth quirked. "This is the most attention you've paid me all week."

"My father is a huge classical music buff. He played Beethoven and Rimsky-Korsakov for my brother and me from the time we began walking. I took violin lessons, and Ryan played piano. What's your instrument of choice?"

He averted his gaze again. "Cello."

"The string section?" She clasped her hands together. "I adore the rich sound a cello produces."

Andrew gave a tight-lipped smile, grabbed her empty mug, and carried it to the sink. He started to wash it without responding. The water sprayed the metal basin. He wiped the dishcloth around the inside.

Victoria rose and followed him. "Which group did you play with?"

He concentrated on scrubbing the cup. "I was second chair with the Austin Symphony Orchestra for five years."

"Second chair?" She stopped beside him and leaned a hip against the counter. "You must have been good."

He winced. "Not good enough for first chair." After plopping the mug in the drying rack, he wrung out the cloth and spread it on the edge of the sink. "Remember to take another dose of cough syrup before you go to bed. Good night." He headed for the door.

"Wait a minute." Victoria spun, forgetting the cumbersome walking cast on her right foot. She stumbled to the side, arms waving.

Andrew sprang forward and caught her around the waist.

Victoria righted herself. Placing a hand on his arm, she looked into his brown eyes. They pulled on her, addling her thoughts and tangling her tongue. "Th-that could have been bad." She held her body taut. "Thank you."

Andrew studied her. He took a short breath. Swallowed. His mouth drew closer to hers.

Her traitorous heart pounded a familiar rhythm. This was how it reacted the first time he'd kissed her. Would this be the second?

Anticipation tickled, followed quickly by panic. She was his boss. They weren't two strangers flirting at a wedding anymore. Her brain scrambled for something to say.

"W-we should play a duet sometime."

Andrew froze a hair's breadth away from her mouth. "A duet?"

What a strange, unexpected suggestion. Why couldn't she come up with something better? It was hard to think with such an appealing male pressed against her.

She slipped out of his embrace. "I brought my violin." She stuffed her wrinkled shirt into her waistband. "We could form a tiny string section sometime. Canon in D is one of my favorites. Are you familiar with it?"

His head jerked back. "Sorry. I don't play duets anymore." A muscle in his jaw jumped. "Or anything else. You should get more rest." He walked from the kitchen, throwing over his shoulder, "Be sure to take your medicine."

The thump of the front door closing spurred Victoria to action. She limped into the living room and saw him pass by her front window. He didn't look her way.

Was he angry she'd halted the kiss? Her spine stiffened. It would have been inappropriate, ill-advised, unprofessional, and—

She sneezed.

And unsanitary.

Victoria dragged her tired body through the room. Where was that cough syrup? She needed to go to bed.

Chapter Eighteen

Humidity enveloped Victoria's shoulders like a moist towel. She held her arms away from her body and fanned the lapel of her gray corduroy suit jacket. Her purple scarf stuck to her skin. She untied the silky material and tucked it in her pocket. Wrong choice of outfit. How was she supposed to know winters in Sweetheart swung from chilly to soggy without warning?

Other teachers opening car doors wore short sleeves and sandals. Was there a local weather report broadcast she missed? Where did they get the down-low on the fluctuating morning temperatures?

The last remaining remnants of her weekend cold, combined with her broken toe, made navigating the drop-off line difficult. She shuffled along, barely getting one door open with each new car rotation.

"Waaaaaaaaaaaaaaaah."

Victoria pinched the bridge of her nose. A few weeks ago, she'd have gone running at such a distressed wail. But this one sounded too rehearsed. Was she developing a mother's ability to distinguish between the children's cries? Besides, hurrying was next to impossible with the walking cast on her foot.

"Waaaaa-aaaa-aaaa-aaah!" The whine escalated and bounced a little at the end.

Nice touch. Very dramatic. It appeared the weeper wasn't going to calm easily. She helped a girl from the car she was servicing and clunked her way down the line.

A child sprawled on the pavement—face buried in his arms. Ms. Amy stood beside him, her hands fanning the flailing body.

A barrel-chested man in a red flannel shirt climbed from an oversized truck cab. His fuzzy beard twitched. He stomped around the front and bellowed at the teacher. "What did you do to my son?"

Victoria speed-walked as fast as her injury allowed toward the confrontation. She recognized those golden curls vibrating against the concrete. The howling child sprawled on the ground.

Ms. Amy cringed as the bull-sized father loomed. "I-I didn't do anything, sir. H-he threw himself on the pavement."

At her feet, the boy kicked. The man retrieved his son, who fastened onto his dad's tattooed neck with a noisy sob.

The father advanced. "He was fine when he got out of the truck."

"Yes, sir. But he …" Ms. Amy retreated. "He didn't like when I told him to put his phone away. Students aren't allowed to use their devices during school hours and—"

The child let out a heartbroken wail as Victoria joined the group. Micah Crumm. Just as she'd suspected.

"Good morning. I'm Principal Park. May I be of service?"

"I certainly hope so!" The menacing man had the same sandy-colored hair as Micah's, only dirtier. He shifted his weeping son to one arm and gestured at the teacher. "This woman upset my son. He never cries."

Victoria glanced at the boy peeking around his father's neck—a distinct twinkle in his eye, even as he wound up for another howl.

She nodded at him. "Hello, Micah."

"Um," Ms. Amy cowered, "to be honest, he acts this way often."

"Are you calling my boy a crybaby?" The veins on the dad's neck stood out.

Victoria took a breath. This wasn't going to be pretty. She placed an arm between them, nudged Ms. Amy back, and stepped in front of the father. "On the contrary, sir. I've witnessed your son throw fits on two separate occasions since I took this job, both times without legitimate provocation. This morning will make the third."

"See there." He gripped Micah tighter. "You made him cry three times. I still got to take my other kid to school." He motioned to the back seat, where a teenage boy slumped without a seatbelt as his thumbs tapped his phone at lightning speed. "And now we're gonna be late. What kind of operation are you running?"

Victoria remained serene. "One where we expect everyone to follow the rules, from the children to the parents. Students aren't allowed to use their phones in school. It should be stored in his backpack, and Micah knows this. If you wish to discuss it further, I'd be happy to talk with you in my office."

The father towered above her. He shoved his face down, his nose almost touching hers, with Micah drooping between the two of them. The colorful response he offered wasn't fit for the ears of a child or anyone else.

The corner of Victoria's mouth lifted. If he thought a few curse words frightened her, he obviously hadn't heard she grew up in New York—Queens, to be exact. Her four-letter education began early, and she could probably enlighten him on a few new ones. She wouldn't. But this man was fortunate her father was a God-fearing minister who'd taught her how to hold her tongue.

Victoria stared up at him, neck aching from the uncomfortable angle. She waited until he ran out of steam, then wiped a trace of spittle from her cheek. "If your unfortunate tirade is over, I'll repeat my offer. You're welcome to come to my office and discuss the situation. Otherwise, I must ask you to leave. Your truck is blocking the car line, and the parents need to get to work."

Father and son gawked at her. Speechless.

"I imagine you also have to be somewhere, Mr. Crumm. If you'd prefer to schedule a conference for a more convenient time, please call the front desk."

Victoria placed her hands under Micah's arms and gently took him from his father's grasp. "Come on, Micah. I'll take you to class. You must be sweating in this unpleasant heat." She held the boy and placed an arm around the teacher. "You come too, Ms. Amy. It's past sign-in time. There's no reason to suffer out here in the humidity."

She strode away like a confident general, even with the limp from her war wound. But inside, she whispered a silent prayer. This was Texas after all. Didn't everyone and their mother own a gun?

Ronnie dashed into the music room and stopped in front of Andrew's desk. "Lord, help!"

"Good morning, my lovely." He smiled. "To what do I owe the pleasure of this visit?"

"Outside." She gasped, hands on her knees. "Principal Park." Her chest heaved. "That crazy father. The crummy guy. He's—"

Andrew raced from the classroom before she finished. After sprinting down the hallway, he reached the double glass door entrance and slammed his hands into one of the push bars.

Victoria stood on the other side, Micah in her arms and a quaking Ms. Amy at her side.

"Are you all right?" He scanned her body and checked if anyone was following them.

No sign of the angry parent.

"We're okay." She gave a strained smile.

"Thanks to you, Ms. Park." Ms. Amy's voice wobbled. "I don't know what I'd have done if you hadn't come. I thought he was going to hit me. That ... that—"

"Shhh!" Victoria cut her glance to the boy. "Micah, why don't you go with Mr. Z? He'll take you to your friends."

Andrew reached out and took the uncharacteristically quiet boy from her. As Andrew walked away, Victoria gave Ms. Amy a brief, awkward pat on the back.

"Don't worry," Victoria said. "I've already begun the process of hiring a security guard to be present during the school day. You won't have to deal with such unpleasantness again."

The pre-K teacher broke into sobs.

"Mr. Z." Micah looked up. "Ms. Bark is tough. I like her."

He hefted the child a little higher. "Me too, Micah. Me too."

Andrew delivered the cheeky boy to his classroom and returned to the front of the school, but Victoria was gone. Maybe he could find her.

Heading for the front office, he approached Ronnie. "Have you—"

"Good morning, Andrew!" a lilting voice called behind him.

Belinda sashayed in his direction. The blue-and-gold splashes of color on her dress resembled a Vincent van Gogh painting. She stopped at his side.

"Hey." He gestured to her clothes. "Nice outfit. Very suitable for an art teacher."

"Thank you." She showed both rows of teeth. "The kids are learning about Impressionism."

"How appropriate." Andrew turned back to Ronnie. "Have you—"

"Ms. Park marched that way carrying a trash bag." The secretary pointed to the outside glass doors.

He laughed. "Are you a mind reader?"

"No. You're just predictable. Whenever you get that expression on your face, it means you're looking for our principal."

Belinda leaned into their conversation. "What expression?"

Ronnie's smile turned smug. "Frustrated. Emotional. Interested. It's a combination."

Belinda's eyes narrowed at Andrew.

He rubbed his jaw. "If you ladies will please excuse me." He left without explanation and headed for the doors Ronnie indicated.

Their observant secretary had his number. All the descriptions she gave applied to him in spades.

Frustrated.

Emotional.

And definitely interested.

Andrew exited and made a circuit around the building. He soon reached the playground, where a kindergarten class was enjoying an early morning recess. Victoria traveled the perimeter by the swing set.

She hobbled with a trash bag in hand. After plucking a gum wrapper from the grass, she added it to her collection.

Children ran by, but she kept her focus pointed at the ground.

Andrew shook his head. She had a broken foot and a cold. What would it take to make this woman stop working? Drawing closer, he noticed Sophie running toward Victoria.

"Ms. Park!" The young girl's joyful voice called out. Wooden mulch flew as the child skidded to a stop. She stared up at the principal.

Victoria bent down an inch. "Yes? Did you need something?"

Sophie twisted her foot in the mulch. "Can I give you a hug again?"

Andrew moved closer, interested in Victoria's response. She didn't seem like the hugging type. But it was hard to say *no* to lovable Sophie.

"Yes." Victoria nodded. "You can hug me, sweetie."

A small smile lit Sophie's face. She stepped forward, wrapped her arms around the principal, and squeezed with youthful abandon.

Victoria gave the girl a hesitant, one-armed squeeze in return. She managed a stiff "Thank you."

Sophie ran off to play. Victoria turned and spotted him. He crossed his arms.

"What?" Pink spread across her cheeks.

Andrew shrugged a shoulder. "You could use some hug lessons."

"Are you offering?"

Was he offering? He certainly wasn't averse to the idea. Before he responded, she stuck a hand in the air.

"Never mind. I didn't mean"—she checked her phone—"forget it. I have a parent conference in five minutes." She spun in the direction of the admin wing.

"Principal Park."

She hesitated and faced him. "Yes?"

Andrew didn't answer right away. The sounds of creaky swings and children squealing filled the silence. The right corner of his lips quirked. "If you decide to stay after school, I'm an excellent hugging tutor." He almost winked at her. His eye didn't actually close, but his flirtatious intent must have been obvious.

Her hand clenched around the trash bag. She left without responding. As Victoria limp-marched away, she grabbed her white, button-down shirt and fanned it from her body.

He must be getting to her.

It was about time.

He couldn't be the only one wondering what might happen if they finished what they'd started at the wedding.

"Hey, Mr. Z!" Micah skipped up while tugging at the neckline of his T-shirt. "It's so hot out!"

Andrew's lips curled in a self-deprecating smirk. Perhaps it wasn't his charm but the Texas humidity getting to the aloof Ms. Park. Was he alone in this attraction?

Chapter Nineteen

Victoria woke before sunrise and stretched in bed, staring at the ceiling. What was she doing? Wasting her life in this small town. Working a job with no hopes for advancement. Flirting with her next-door neighbor.

Technically, she wasn't flirting *with* him. She hadn't reciprocated his teasing advances since becoming principal. But Andrew grew harder to resist by the day. And his sweet stint as her self-appointed nurse over the weekend made it all the more difficult.

Old Blue screeched from the backyard. At least she hadn't given the crotchety rooster the satisfaction of waking her. She sat up and swung her feet to the floor. It was time to stop being a bystander and make something happen. She grabbed her laptop bag from the chair in the corner.

Time to look for a way out of Sweetheart.

Victoria spent an hour updating her resume and researching universities. Higher education was where she belonged, not comforting crying children and facing off with recalcitrant parents. The alarm on her watch jingled. She dressed in a hurry and climbed into her borrowed car for the short trip to work.

She drove through the quiet streets of Sweetheart. The windows of Heavenly Roasters were dark. Still too early. The morning must be battled without an espresso. She stopped at the town's lone stoplight at the end of Main Street. It flashed red. Where she came from, they would never dare to turn off the lights, but the locals must have deemed it unnecessary for the few rowdy souls who stayed awake past midnight.

Making a left on Colter Avenue, Victoria passed three churches in the two-mile stretch to the school. Did Sweetheart hold enough citizens to fill them all? Her father's small congregation in Queens contained fewer than fifty people, but he'd managed to keep the doors open for the past thirty-five years. It must take a special kind of guts to be a minister.

Her conscience pinged. Dad had been after her for years to pick a church. Any church.

It's not like she'd rejected God. She was a Christian. But she'd been busy with the university. Staff meetings. Weekend study groups. Grading papers. Favors for the dean.

Work consumed her life.

And where did it get you?

The quiet Voice whispered in her head.

She cast a glance at the sky, where the faintest tinge of light was starting to appear.

"Acknowledged," she spoke aloud. "It was all for nothing, God. I would have been better served to spend my Sundays in church."

Victoria made a right at the Stop sign and entered the empty school parking lot. She pulled into the spot reserved for the principal in the first row near the main entrance and switched off the ignition. After grabbing her purse from the passenger seat, she exited the car and closed the door. A slash of purple caught her eye. She squinted in the ever-growing light of dawn.

Painted on the school wall, the face of a black crow stared back.

"What in the world?" She hurried across the dew-covered grass and studied the graffiti.

The crow's mouth opened wide, razor-sharp teeth poking from the beak, a purple scarf tied around its neck. Adorning the bricks above its head, a speech balloon held the words "Move down, please!!!"

She clenched her teeth at the three exclamation points. The over-punctuated dialogue was an obvious reference to her, but that hardly mattered. The real issue was how much distraction it would cause at morning drop-off.

Could it be cleaned before the students arrived?

Victoria raced inside the school as fast as her broken toe allowed and raided the janitor's closet. She grabbed a mop, bucket, sponges, industrial cleaner, and anything else in sight. Returning to the painting, she peeled off her suit coat, tossed it on the ground, and scrubbed for all she was worth.

Half an hour later, she'd barely made a dent. The paint had faded, but the bird remained intact. Its words were still legible. Victoria checked her watch. Less than ten minutes before teachers started arriving.

The biting odor from the pungent cleaner pricked her nostrils. A ghost of a headache knocked. Her arms ached from the fruitless scouring.

She dropped to the ground. Her eyes stung. Was it the overpowering scent or an oncoming emotional breakdown? Not the second one. She didn't have time for crying. Could she find a piece of bulletin board paper large enough to cover the wretched crow before anyone else saw it?

~

ANDREW DROVE THROUGH THE STAFF ENTRANCE LATER THAN NORMAL. He kept a steadying hand on the donut boxes on the passenger seat and drummed his fingers against the cardboard. Buying a treat for the teacher break room had been a great idea. But getting stuck in the drive-thru line behind a customer who changed her order three times was a danger to his mental health.

Would Victoria give him an earful for being late? She wasn't the kind to be swayed by a jelly-filled bribe.

He cut through the stretch of student drop-off cars to reach the lot. The sheer length surprised him. Why were they backed out to the street? He expected Victoria to be hopping along the sidewalk, ready to open every door by herself. But she was nowhere in sight.

Andrew chose a space at the end of a row, parked, and walked toward the school with boxes in hand. Vehicles inched forward. Drivers hung their arms out the windows with phones pointed at the building.

Had something happened to a student?

A crowd congregated near the wall by the entrance. He approached and peered over their heads. A painted crow filled the bricks with the words "Move down, please" and three exclamation points.

The inference was obvious.

No wonder the parents acted like rubberneckers driving by a traffic accident. They laughed as they videoed the graffiti and stopped their cars to talk to the teachers opening the doors. The pictures they took were probably halfway to the county line by now.

He entered the building. Belinda leaned on the front counter, whispering to Ronnie. The teacher bounced on her toes. Her short skirt with multicolored paintbrushes printed on the hem vibrated.

"Oh, thank heavens you're here!" Belinda locked on his arm as soon as he reached them. "We were just wondering what to do. Such a crazy way to start the morning."

The secretary stood and placed her hands on the counter. "The parents are driving two miles an hour through the parking lot. The kids are laughing their heads off. And Principal Park is nowhere to be found." Ronnie shook her head. "Strange. I supposed she was made of sterner stuff. I didn't expect her to run away and hide because of a prank."

Belinda smirked. "I guess she's human after all."

"Don't count her out yet." Andrew extricated himself from her grasp. "I bet she's trying to figure out who did this." He passed the donuts to Ronnie. "If you two will excuse me, I need to get my lesson plans ready."

He walked to the music room, switched on his computer, and stared out the window. Thunder grumbled as gray clouds roiled overhead—a fitting forecast.

He imagined Victoria must be spitting nails over the vandalism.

Where was she anyway?

Chapter Twenty

A persistent rain pelted The Brunch Café's window. Victoria sat in a booth, facing away from the room. The normal buzz of the breakfast crowd had dropped to whispers the moment she entered the restaurant.

Had everyone heard about the graffiti?

Her head pounded like the oversized drops on the glass. She rubbed her temples, and a sharp scent invaded her nostrils. She sniffed her fingers and blanched. The chemical smell lingered. Black paint coated the underside of her nails.

Ryan and Katherine arrived, shaking the moisture from their jackets. Why couldn't her brother come alone? Did he have to take his wife everywhere?

Newlyweds.

Victoria waved the couple over. She ignored the surreptitious glances of the diners surrounding them and filled in her brother on the vandalism. When she finished, Ryan clicked his tongue, picked up a menu, and motioned for the waitress.

"The rain stopped," he said.

How could he be so dismissive? Didn't he realize this was a crisis?

"They painted on the school?" Her sister-in-law's gaze sharpened. The booth's red vinyl bench creaked as she shifted forward. "Someone left graffiti on the walls?"

"Yes." Victoria drummed her black-tipped fingers. "You expect this kind of problem in a high school. But elementary?" She slapped the shiny tabletop. "It's not right!"

Her brother put down his menu. "Oh boy."

Katherine gave the table an equally resounding smack. "No it's not!"

Ryan sighed. "Here we go."

His wife ignored him and dug in her purse. "We have to do something. Did the security cameras catch it?"

"That's the worst part," Victoria said. "The school doesn't have security cameras."

Katherine stilled. "None at all?"

"Not even inside. I know this is a safe, small town, but it's the twenty-first century. A public facility for children requires security cameras."

Katherine pulled out her phone and typed. "I'm texting the school board now. They should put this on the agenda for the next meeting. Our children deserve better. Some paint-happy idiot is defacing our town property, and it could have been solved easily if we'd installed the proper equipment."

Victoria retrieved her own phone. "I'll research the best systems. You can present my findings to the board."

Katherine nodded while she texted. "Don't worry, Vic. This flagrant destruction of school property will end. I'll make sure of it."

The owner, Susanna, approached their table with a tray and set three cups of fragrant, black coffee in front of them. "Did y'all decide what to eat?"

Her brother ordered for them as Victoria clicked on a promising web link.

After scanning the different options, she turned her phone around and held it in front of Katherine. "Here's the best option. Reviewers recommend it, but it isn't pricey."

Katherine nodded. "Text me the information. I'll call the school board."

She poked her husband in the arm. He slid out of the booth, let her pass, and sat back down.

Ryan propped his chin in his hand. "Thanks a lot, Vic. She'll be awake half the night making this happen."

Victoria looked through the café's window. Katherine stood outside, holding the phone to her ear. She paced without a care for the water splashing in the puddles with her every step.

Victoria pursed her lips and nodded. "I'm beginning to understand what you see in her."

Ryan lifted his cup in salute. "She's like black coffee—hard to take at first, but now I can't wake up without her."

"Bleggghhhh." She waved both hands in front of her. "Too much information, little brother. It floors me to hear you utter such sentimental mush. I remember the days, make that years, when I had no clue who you were dating. You didn't even mention them."

"Because they weren't worth mentioning." Ryan's smile softened as he watched Katherine, who was punctuating her talk with emphatic jerks of her hand. "I bet you've never met anyone like my wife."

"Most definitely."

A few weeks ago, Victoria might have added she never wanted to meet anyone like Katherine again. But her sister-in-law grew on a person once they got past the un-sugared comments and passionate speeches about her latest crusade.

Victoria agreed with her brother. Katherine *was* like a strong cup of coffee, something Victoria considered a perk of life. She admitted having such an honest do-gooder in the family raised the Park brand. But she hoped her future nieces and nephews would inherit their father's temperament.

Chapter Twenty-One

Andrew paced the duplex's front porch, eyes focused on the driveway. Victoria was noticeably absent the entire school day. Other teachers had joked about how peaceful it was, but he'd found it hard to concentrate on music classes.

Was she upset?

Had she taken the graffiti personally?

Of course she had. How could she not when someone portrayed her as a shrieking crow? It didn't state her name, but the intention was obvious.

The gossipy Mrs. Biddle happened to be volunteering at the school. Thanks to her, the word spread like milk on a pre-K lunch table. By noon, the whole town had heard, and parents arrived early for dismissal to take selfies with the painting.

Andrew sat on the steps. He threaded his fingers together between his knees. His foot beat a nervous tattoo against the concrete. Ten seconds later, he jumped up.

Had she packed her bags and headed for New York?

He ruffled the hair at the back of his neck and kicked a stray pebble. A rattling sounded. Victoria's rickety sedan creaked into the driveway, the chassis griping at every dip in the ground.

A smile started deep down in his stomach and exploded across his face. Andrew bounced off the porch. A whistle formed on his lips, but he suppressed it. She might not be in the best mood after her unpleasant morning surprise.

Victoria parked in the driveway and climbed from the car. Her purse hung from her slumped shoulder. She dragged a laptop bag from the passenger seat and shut the door. He noted the faint black smudges on her fingertips from trying to remove the graffiti. Her plastic walking cast thumped as she headed his way. She didn't spot him until they almost collided.

"Oh." She reared back. "Excuse me. I didn't see you."

"Understandable." Andrew took the bag from her hand. "You had an unexpected surprise this morning."

"To put it mildly." She clunked her way up the steps. "My nerves are stretched tighter than my violin's strings. All I want to do is sit on the couch and die."

He followed close behind. "You missed the school day."

Victoria pulled her keys from her purse and inserted one in the lock. "I doubt the school missed me back. They must have been relieved the old crow was gone."

She slapped the door open and entered without closing it. That was invitation enough for him. Andrew crossed the threshold and placed her bag next to the cough syrup on the coffee table. Only an inch of sticky red liquid remained in the bottle.

Victoria collapsed on the couch and leaned her head against the cushion.

He hovered in the middle of the living room. "Are you going to turn on the Beethoven and relax?"

Her eyelids closed. "I don't have the strength. Just tell the undertaker he can pick me up here in the morning."

While Andrew appreciated her ability to maintain a sense of humor, he suspected there was hurt mixed with the sarcasm. She'd worked from sunup to sundown to improve Sweetheart Elementary and got nothing but grief in return.

An unexpected idea popped into his brain.

He shoved the thought away, but it circled back like a boomerang.

Didn't she deserve a break? Every teacher at the school, with the exception of the adoring Ms. Amy, had made Victoria's life difficult. He owed her some compensation.

"Be right back."

Andrew went to his apartment and opened the closet door. His cello sat in the same spot, piles of junk blocking the way. He dug through the miscellaneous items and maneuvered out the hard-shell case, which was covered in a fine layer of dust.

He returned to Victoria's place with the instrument. Eyes closed, she remained in the same spot he'd left her. Andrew popped the metal clasps on the case and withdrew the cello. The polished wood gleamed a warm coffee brown as if glad to meet him after so long.

He carried a chair closer to the couch, sat, and grabbed the bow from the case. After taking a small metal container of rosin in hand, he coated the hair of the bow. The familiar whooshing sound was one he'd heard many times. He twisted the cello pegs to tighten the strings, and ran a few test strokes. When he finished tuning, he looked at Victoria.

She was no longer inert. Her body tilted forward. Her eyes pointed at the cello. The emotion of a proud parent filled him. He exhaled and began to play.

Rich music filled the small space. After a year without touching a bow, he'd expected his skills to be rusty, but they returned like the lyrics to an old, familiar song. The years of lessons and study and countless hours of practicing hadn't deserted him.

Andrew performed one of his favorites about a peaceful, sunny pasture on the English coast. Over a stone wall, the ocean glimmered in the distance, where a tall ship with sails cut through the white-capped waves. This wasn't a story the composer intended with the piece. Andrew always imagined a setting to go with the music he played. His childhood instructor had taught him this trick to make the sound come alive.

After the day Victoria had endured, she could use a vacation in the country. His fingers slid up and down the strings, painting a melodic picture to soothe her soul. He silently whispered a prayer for God to comfort her.

His song approached the final measures. The horsehair drew across the strings in one last, drawn-out stroke. The final note hummed and faded away.

No applause. It was the expected reaction when he played for an audience.

Andrew glanced up and froze. Victoria's dark eyes glistened. She took a deep breath, pointing her gaze at the ceiling. Her mouth moved, but it was a moment before words formed.

"That was ..." She cleared her throat. "That was—" Victoria's eyes squeezed shut. "Why can't I think of the right word? *Beautiful* is too trite." She murmured through quivery lips, "Thank you."

The back of his neck heated. Forget standing ovations in a giant concert hall. Her simple words were the highest praise he'd ever received.

"Aw, shucks." Andrew stretched. "You don't have to cry about it."

"I never cry." She settled back on the couch, her body limp. "The Austin Symphony must miss you."

He took a soft cloth from the case and wiped the shiny wood. "Please don't mention my past experience to people. I keep it under wraps."

"Why should you be ashamed?"

"I'm not ashamed." He rubbed the side of his nose. "I'm afraid Pastor Thibodeaux will ask me to join the worship team. He knows I play several instruments, but I really don't want to lug my heavy cello case to church every week." He gave an exaggerated groan as he lifted the instrument, placed it in the case, and secured the bow with its clip.

"Understood." Victoria's eyebrows crinkled. "How does a classical cellist wind up employed as an elementary music teacher in this tiny town?"

Andrew leaned forward, pausing with the attitude of a joke teller about to deliver a punchline. "Katherine. Bruno. Park."

Victoria laughed. "I should have guessed."

"Yes, you should have. Your sister-in-law is a force only God and her husband can reckon with. I gave a talk about faith in the arts at a conference my Austin church hosted for Christian leaders and influencers. During the speech, I happened to mention how tired I'd grown of the big city and said I wished for a simpler life."

"You don't have to tell me what happened next."

"Yep. Katherine made a beeline for me after my class and spent half an hour extolling the joys of small-town living. I agreed to visit, more to get her to stop talking than anything. But after I saw Sweetheart for myself, I was a goner. I felt at home for the first time in my life. People welcomed me like a long-lost son."

"Welcomed." Victoria's jaw tightened. "Must've been nice."

Tension replaced the relaxed atmosphere. Victoria kneaded

the muscles in her back. "Speaking of my sister-in-law, I spent the day with Katherine, developing a counterstrategy for finding the vandal."

"Counterstrategy?" Andrew's lips twitched.

Victoria ignored his amusement. "Katherine's going to push the board to fund security cameras for the school. She's asked them to call a special meeting to expedite the process."

"Not much hope of that." Andrew shut his case and flipped the metal clasps. He grabbed the handle and stood. "Turtles move faster than the board."

"Oh, I don't know." Victoria grinned as she joined him. "Katherine will provide enough heat to make them run."

"You may be right."

They smiled at each other for the space of a second until it became awkward.

"Uh"—Andrew pointed at the door—"until tomorrow."

He left her and headed to his apartment. Inside, he walked to the closet and paused.

He'd played since the age of seven. To say the Zimmerman family was driven in their ambitions was putting it politely. Both of his brothers achieved valedictorian status in high school and college. But not him. They went on to earn doctorates in their chosen fields of medicine and chemistry. Although his father never outright stated it, Andrew sensed he was disappointed in his artsy son.

For years, Andrew practiced six hours a day, seven days a week. Striving to attain the musical equivalent of ultimate success—and always failing. When he packed his instrument in the case and shoved it in the back of the closet, he left a part of himself behind. For months, he'd dreamed of playing and awoke with his fingers moving in the air over imaginary strings.

Andrew pushed away the past. He set the case on the floor,

lifted the lid, and took hold of the cello's slender neck. It settled in place like an old friend shaking his hand. He stroked the fingerboard.

The frustration of failing to achieve the principal cellist title had driven him from the music world. He spouted platitudes to his students about following their dreams, but he'd given up on his own. He was incompetent—in high school, college, adult life. No matter which orchestra he played with or how hard he practiced, he never attained that lead position.

Andrew rubbed the tips of his fingers together. After a year without holding a bow, his calluses had grown soft. The pads ached where he'd pressed on the thick, metal cello strings.

And he loved it.

It was all thanks to Victoria. Something about her made him want to try again. To be better.

Worthy of her.

Chapter Twenty-Two

A cloudless sunrise painted the horizon a burnished orange with a canopy of subtle, blue shades hovering overhead. Victoria sat in the school parking lot with a café mocha in hand. She whispered a quick prayer of thanks that Heavenly Roasters had been open. Although the coffee shop posted set hours, there was no guarantee. If Amy's mom didn't feel like opening at seven, she didn't.

Victoria took an extra-large swig of coffee, followed by another. She braced herself to face the graffiti. The sweet concert from Andrew the previous night had bolstered her spirits, but her emotions felt tender, like a freshly scraped knee.

She exited the car and steeled her resolve as she approached the building, expecting to be greeted by the ugly crow. Instead, a fresh coat of reddish-brown paint glistened in the early morning sunlight. It didn't match the bricks exactly, but she much preferred it to the mean-spirited caricature.

Victoria had planned to ask the custodian to do the exact same thing until they properly cleaned the wall. It was item one on her to-do list for the day. Did the man anticipate her request?

As she entered the building, a clanging sound drew her attention from the right hallway. She walked as quietly as her cumbersome cast would allow and peeked around the corner. Andrew stood by his classroom with a small stepladder. He disappeared inside and returned a moment later to grab a can of paint sitting on the floor.

Victoria ducked back. She pressed a hand to her racing heart. Forget chocolate and roses. This was the most meaningful gift she'd ever received.

How could she thank him?

Launching herself into his arms and shouting her gratitude, although appealing, was out of the question.

Victoria tiptoe-clunked away to her office until she could decide on the best course of action. But in the end, she chose the uninspired idea of buying him lunch.

Anonymously.

She didn't want Mrs. Biddle getting wind of it and spreading more rumors. Victoria made the short drive to Rosa's Taqueria at lunchtime and bought two flauta plates with rice and charro beans. She'd once overheard Andrew raving about them in a conversation with Ronnie.

After returning to school, she stored the bag with the lunch containers inside her office until an ideal time presented itself to sneak the food into his classroom. Victoria studied the schedule. Andrew's last class before his break should be leaving.

She walked down the hall to check. Instead of empty, there were noisy children crowded around the music room door. Victoria approached the disturbance.

At the classroom threshold, Sophie stood with her face

crumpled, tears streaking her cheeks. Victoria hurried to her side. She shooed the students away to give them some room.

"What's wrong, sweetie?" The endearment came more naturally these days.

Lips trembling, the child shook her head and refused to answer.

A young classmate peeked over Sophie's shoulder. "She doesn't want to leave music."

Victoria's eyes rolled halfway up, but she stopped them. "Is that the reason?" She crouched in front of the little girl. "You don't want to leave music?"

A fervent nod came as more tears spilled.

Victoria glanced at Sophie's distracted teacher, Mrs. Dole, trying to herd the children into some semblance of a line. It looked like Victoria would have to figure this out herself. She raised a hesitant hand, paused, and let it drop.

"Don't worry. You have music class again in a few days, right?"

Another silent nod.

She straightened. "Then please go back to class. You'll see Mr. Z soon."

Sophie's shoulders rounded.

Victoria sighed. It appeared her lackluster pep talk hadn't convinced the child. Was there any female immune to the charms of Sweetheart's gorgeous music teacher?

Andrew poked his head out of the classroom. "What's the problem, people? We have half a class waiting to exit."

Victoria leaned close. "Your biggest fan is heartbroken at the thought of leaving you."

He gave a short chuckle, moved around in front of Sophie, and lowered to her height.

"Hey, honey. Are you sad?"

"Yes," the girl squeaked.

"I understand. I used to get super bummed when I left music class. How about I make you a deal?"

He drew her away from the other students and whispered something in her ear.

Sophie's face brightened. A smile appeared. "You promise?"

He kissed his thumb and held out his pinky. "Promised and sealed."

Sophie hooked her pinky with his. "Deal."

She scrambled into line.

Mrs. Dole gave Andrew a grateful salute. The kindergarten traffic jam cleared, and Sophie's class left.

Victoria crossed her arms. "What kind of bribe made her dry up so fast?"

"More music."

"I don't understand."

"You will." He whistled as he reentered the classroom. "See you later, Principal Park."

ANDREW SWUNG BY THE MUSIC ROOM TO FETCH HIS GUITAR AFTER end-of-day dismissal. He grasped the case's handle and strolled to the side of the school under the pine trees. As expected, Sophie sat with Victoria, whose leg with the walking cast stretched in front of her. She held a book in hand. Her cultured voice read the story aloud.

"Hmmmm." She paused in the middle of the story and pointed to the page. "I need a little help. What's this word, Sophie?"

The girl scooted closer and studied the book. "'Pu-ppy.'"

"Good job." Victoria didn't pile the praise on, but she gave an affirming nod. "'The puppy jumped in the basket and—'" She paused as he approached.

Sophie jumped to her feet. "Mr. Z!"

"Hey, Sophie." Andrew placed the case on the ground, unzipped it, and pulled out his guitar. "I'm here to keep my promise."

"Yay!" She clapped.

He sat on the far end of the bench and nodded to her empty seat. "Sit down. I'll give you and Ms. Park a special concert."

Sophie plopped between them.

Victoria eyed him over the girl's head. "Was this the bribe you offered her today?"

"Of course." He rested the guitar on his leg and strummed a chord. "The only way to stop someone from missing music is with more music. Any requests?"

Victoria closed the book and settled it on her lap.

Andrew's gaze dropped to the picture of the cartoon puppy on the cover. He snapped his fingers. "I've got the perfect tune. It goes with your story. I bet you both know this song." He slipped his pick from under the guitar strings, began a rousing double-time strum, and sang, *"There was a farmer had a dog, and Bingo was his name-o.* Sing it, Sophie!"

"B-I-N-G-O!" she shouted.

Sophie and he performed with enthusiasm. Victoria clapped along but didn't join them in singing.

Andrew kept playing. "Come on, Ms. Park. Join us. *B-I-N-G-O."*

Her lips parted. A tiny sound issued out, too soft to be heard.

Sophie grabbed her hand as she sang. Her eyes sparkled. "You can do it, Ms. Park. Sing strong!"

Victoria gulped. But she sang louder.

Andrew winced.

The woman's pitch was flat as a two-by-four. Who would have guessed? The perfectionist Principal Park was tone-deaf.

Sophie didn't mind. While holding Victoria's hand, she bounced to the beat, her smile so wide it covered half her face. They finished "Bingo," and Andrew switched to a rock and roll version of "Yankee Doodle."

The three of them sang for five minutes until Sophie's mom drove into the parking lot with a cheerful honk.

Sophie's lower lip jutted. "I don't want to leave music," she wailed.

Victoria's eyes closed. "Wasn't this what instigated our jam session in the first place?"

Andrew waved a finger at the child. "Listen, young lady. Your mom might feel sad if she thought you didn't want to see her. There will be plenty of time for singing another day."

"Promise?" She kissed her thumb and poked out her pinky.

"Promise." He completed their ritual, stood, and put his guitar in the case.

Sophie threw her arms around Victoria's neck. "Bye, Ms. Park."

Victoria stiffened for a second, loosened, and patted the girl's back with both hands. "Goodbye, Sophie."

Another horn burst. Mrs. Harris gestured from inside her car, the front passenger window lowered. She hollered, "Sophie, hurry. We need to visit your grandma." The woman gave Victoria a thumbs-up. "Thank you, Ms. Park!"

Victoria walked Sophie to the car and waved as the two drove off.

Andrew waited until she turned around to shake his head with an exaggerated "Tsk-tsk."

"What?" she asked.

"It's time for that lesson." He checked first to make sure no one else was in sight. Everyone had either gone home or was inside the building. Andrew gathered Victoria to him.

As with Sophie, she stiffened.

"Don't misunderstand." He kept his tone impersonal. "I'm gifting you a free hug lesson. It comes with the song." He tapped a hand on her back. "Being a male teacher, I'm very careful about instigating hugs with the students. I try to do more fist bumps and high fives, but you can be more comfortable granting them a cuddle. Note the position of my arms. They are overlapping, not barely reaching around you."

"You're ridiculous," she scoffed, even as she stayed in his light embrace.

Andrew held her a little closer. "After you've hugged someone, apply the slightest amount of pressure for comfort. Like a weighted blanket. Patting them gently is fine."

He demonstrated by tapping his fingers ever so lightly. Victoria's body relaxed beneath his. Her chin tilted so it rested on his shoulder. Her small hands, warm and slender, settled at his waist.

Fire shot from his toes to his earlobes. Any altruistic thoughts took a swift left turn.

Andrew jerked away and moved out of her hold. "Not bad. Do that with Sophie the next time she hugs you." He turned, released a breath, and zipped up his case. "Thanks for the flautas. They were delicious."

"How did you know they were from me?"

He straightened. "I have my sources. Good afternoon, ma'am."

He speed-walked away with a cheery but totally fake whistle. What he wanted to do was go and hold his head under the water fountain like the boys did after recess. His motives had been entirely pure at the start of the hug lesson. Victoria Park required help connecting with the children at school. But her soft body pressed against his, and her tentative response skewed his intentions. All of a sudden, he wasn't Andrew Zimmerman the hug tutor. He was Andrew Zimmerman the man.

Principal Park loved to keep things strictly business. And his pounding pulse was miles away from professional.

Chapter Twenty-Three

Victoria entered the office and chucked her clipboard on the desk. Stalking to the window, she crossed her arms and surveyed the scene. Parents gathered around the wall by the entrance, phones lifted. Behind them stretched a brand-new piece of graffiti. This time, the head resembled a crow, but the rest was a female body in a suit with an oversize megaphone raised to its beak. If anyone doubted the crow's identity, there was no longer any question.

Another speech bubble declared, "Wait your turn!"

Micah's dad squatted in front of the painting, bushy beard vibrating with laughter, as his teen son took a picture. The man flexed tattooed muscles in a power pose and guffawed.

A few people craned their necks in the direction of her office window, so she scurried away from the glass. Morning drop-off had been torture, enduring the questioning glances of teachers and parents. She'd manufactured a stoic expression and soldiered on.

The school board was dragging its feet on funding the security cameras. She'd pay for them herself if it were just a matter of expense, but she also required their permission to install them on the building. Good old protocol.

"What do I do now, God?"

She was consulting the Almighty a lot more of late. Hardly surprising when life was one lion's den after another. She sank onto her chair, slumped on the desk, and moaned. A knock on the door brought up her head. Her sister-in-law burst into the office with her brother right behind.

"Vic!" Katherine said. "Are you okay?"

"Of course." Victoria eyed them both. "What are you doing here?"

Ryan joined his wife. "Mrs. Biddle stopped by the mayor's office and informed us about the new graffiti."

"What!" Victoria stood. "How did she find out? I didn't see her at school."

"Biddle has spies everywhere." Ryan crossed to the window.

Victoria half laughed, half whimpered as she came around the desk, rubbing the bridge of her nose. "Why bother with security cameras? Let's ask Mrs. Biddle who the vandal is. She probably already knows."

Katherine shook her head. "If she did, the whole town would know. What are we going to do about this?"

Victoria looked through splayed fingers at her sister-in-law. "I'm new to small-town life. Is the mayor always this involved in the elementary school's problems?"

"This isn't about the school." Katherine took her by the hand. "It's about family."

Victoria felt the unexpected urge to embrace her. Maybe Andrew's hug lessons were working. Instead, she sat on one of the chairs facing her desk. "In that case, Sis, what do you suggest?"

Katherine perched on the matching chair. "You painted

over the last crow, and the delinquent struck again, right? I say we set a trap."

"A trap? How?"

"Paint over the new bird right away. It's a matter of pride with this thug. I bet he or she will come the same night and create a new one. But this time, we'll be here to catch them."

"You're not serious." Ryan turned to study Victoria and his wife.

Katherine snapped her fingers. "Remember when we couldn't figure out who was sabotaging Lanette Johnson's political campaign? We caught the guy by guessing where he'd strike next and staking out the place."

He crossed his arms. "I thought *that* was a bad idea too. But I went along to keep you out of trouble."

"It worked, didn't it?" She smirked. "We got footage of him setting fire to a poster."

"Then how about keeping the simplest part of the plan?" Ryan walked across the room, squatted between their chairs, and faced Victoria. "Rather than waiting for the school board to set up official security cameras, why not leave one camera recording the spot? A cell phone would work. Hide it in here. Your office window has a perfect vantage. We can check the footage in the morning."

She thumped her brother on the chest. "Good suggestion. Why not do both? I can hide nearby—"

Katherine poked her head over Ryan's shoulder. "*We* can hide nearby—"

"And we'll have video proof to back up our eyewitness accounts."

He rubbed his forehead. "What if the vandal doesn't show tonight?"

"Then we watch the next night?"

"And if he still doesn't show?" Her brother stood. "Are you

guys planning to live at the school? Should I buy a tent and sleeping bags?"

"That's ridiculous," Victoria said.

"Exactly!" Ryan pumped a fist in the air. "Take the easy way first. Set up the camera for a few nights. If it doesn't work, hold your slumber party then."

"Careful." Katherine's jaw jutted. "You're starting to sound like a sexist."

He flicked a finger under her chin. "You know me better than that."

They stared at each other in amused adoration about some secret inside joke. Victoria wasn't privy to the punch line, and she didn't want to be.

Standing, she fetched her clipboard from the desk. "Fine. I'll try it your way for three nights." She retrieved a pencil from the holder. "If it doesn't work, I'll sleep at the school until I catch the reprobate."

Katherine's attention returned to her. "Don't you dare leave me out of the exciting stuff."

Victoria smiled. "I wouldn't dream of it."

Ryan plopped on the chair she'd vacated. "Have I missed something? When did you two become besties?"

"You were right." Victoria waggled her head. "We have more in common than we realized. Now if you'll excuse me, I need to find the custodian and tell him to repaint the wall. Again."

A KNOCK LED ANDREW TO HIS APARTMENT DOOR. HE OPENED IT TO find Victoria. A moon the size of Texas filled the sky behind her, and a breeze rustled the oak leaves in the front yard.

His gaze dropped to the small violin case under her arm.

She tucked a loose strand of hair behind her ear. "It's been a rough day, and music relaxes me. But I'm not sure how thin the walls are in this duplex. My neighbors in New York used to complain if I practiced my violin past eight o'clock. Would it bother you if I played for a while?"

"Yes." He kept his face expressionless.

Victoria's mouth opened, closed, and reopened. "I ... I didn't expect that response. Didn't you say you were a night owl? Besides, you're a music teacher."

He allowed a cheeky grin to appear. "I refuse to listen while you have all the fun. Let me grab my cello. We'll make it a duet."

Andrew stepped aside and gestured to the living room. She entered and walked toward the couch.

"Oh, no." He waved a hand. "You'll never get good leverage for playing on those worn-out cushions. Let's go in the kitchen. The chairs are hard, and the acoustics are stellar—just right for a midnight concert."

"It's eleven."

Andrew left the room without responding.

"Sorry." Victoria's voice followed him. "My default setting is always to argue."

He returned with his cello case, and she apologized again. "I'm sorry. I'm a bit cranky."

"Small wonder." He led her into the kitchen, pulled a chair away from the table, and motioned for her to sit. "The second painting was even less flattering than the first. I swear, it kind of looks like you."

She gave a self-deprecating chuckle. "I noticed. Whoever the vandal is, he's talented."

Victoria sat. Andrew settled on the chair he positioned opposite her. They tuned their instruments without speaking and coated their bows with rosin.

Andrew leaned the cello against his chest. The large, wooden body comforted him like a shield. "Any requests?"

She placed the violin on her shoulder and settled her chin on the rest. "Do you know Canon in D?"

He cocked his head. "Would you ask an English professor if he knows the alphabet?"

Andrew began to bow. The slow back-and-forth of the composer's opening notes sang from the instrument like a mother humming a lullaby. Victoria joined on the melody. The high notes rolled from her violin, strengthened by the answering call of his cello.

Her technique was good. Not as advanced as a symphony player's, but she held her bow at the proper angle, and her body swayed to the rhythm, in tune with the piece's emotion. Andrew adjusted to her sound, lessening his volume, and allowing her to take the lead. As they reached the intricate part of the composition, her fingers flew across the strings, sure and dexterous. The cello part wasn't the star of this canon. It repeated over and over, a steady foundation anchoring the violin.

Their music bounced off the tile floor. The cadence created an echo chamber, surrounding them in rich, buttery sounds that melted in a comforting warmth. They approached the coda. Both of them slowed as if they didn't want it to end. Their bows drew as one and held out the final note until it faded away.

Victoria lowered the violin. Her eyes met his. Captivated him.

He didn't move. Didn't breathe. Several feet of space separated them, but the music had drawn their spirits together in unison. The intimate moment rocked his core.

She shot to her feet and scrambled for her case, hands

fumbling. Not bothering to place the violin inside, she shoved the bag under her arm.

"Thanks. I feel much more better. I mean, I'm better feeling." She took a breath. "I. Feel. Better. Good night." Victoria limped to the front door and departed without a backward glance.

Andrew remained seated. A smile crept to his lips.

It wasn't the humidity this time.

He was definitely getting to her.

Chapter Twenty-Four

This boy was getting to her.

Victoria stared at the five-year-old with the half-eaten chocolate bar. Micah Crumm pressed sticky lips together in a determined line. His eyes squinted. He dared to take another giant bite after she'd just told him to put the candy away.

She propped her hands on her hips. "Chocolate is not for breakfast. Save it for later."

"I don't wanna."

Chatty lines of students walked by on their way from morning pledges in the gym. Teachers' lips quivered as they passed. Ronnie sat at the front desk with her chin propped in both hands as if enjoying the show. Why did there have to be an audience for this lose-lose confrontation?

Victoria wanted to snatch the wretched chocolate from his hand. She lightened her tone instead. "Sweetie," she cooed. "Do a good job and put it away. You can eat it at lunch." Her teeth clenched. "Put. It. Away. Now."

"You're mean!" He dashed down the hallway.

Ronnie's chortle did little to help Victoria's temper.

Victoria glared at her. "Thanks for the backup."

The secretary snorted. "I don't have the guts to get between a kindergartner and his candy bar. Props to you for bravery."

"Not that it did any good."

Ronnie graced her with a fond smile. "Sugar, if they had someone with your mettle at the Alamo, they might have won."

"Yeah right." Victoria massaged her back. "I can't even win against a five-year-old. I miss having students over the legal driving age. At least I didn't have to correct their bad eating habits or call them pet names."

Ronnie observed her with a long-suffering expression.

"I admit it." Victoria shrugged. "I'm not good with the children. It's a whole new world for me here. If I'd called one of my students *sweetie* at the university, I might be accused of sexual harassment. Maintaining a proper distance wasn't just to uphold professional boundaries. It was protecting my reputation from a lawsuit."

Ronnie nodded. "I get your point. But that excuse only goes so far. Ignorance can always be fixed. Perhaps you should do some research."

Victoria stepped to the side as a group of pre-K students gabbled their way past her. "Research?"

"Call me crazy. I'm guessing you were one of the kids who studied hard in school. Am I right?"

"Most definitely."

"Then apply that same get-up-and-go to Sweetheart Elementary. If you don't understand the kids, do your homework. Study them. Get after-school tutoring."

"Tutoring?" Victoria laughed. "Does anyone offer a class in how to speak kid?"

Ronnie pointed. "You've got an expert right down the hall.

Andrew Zimmerman is the best teacher I've seen in my thirty years at this school. He's fun and easygoing but doesn't let the students get away with things. And they love him for it." She winked. "I'm going to grab a donut from the break room. Think about what I said. If you want to relate to the children, learn from a master." Ronnie bustled away, pausing every few feet to hug a passing child.

Victoria focused on her own feet. The one encased in a walking cast tapped the floor.

Learn from a master?

It made sense.

But why did the expert have to be the one man in Sweetheart who made her heart ring like a dismissal bell?

Victoria retreated to her office. Though she hated letting anything slide, Micah would get away with an unhealthy breakfast for one morning. The surveillance video awaited her. Even though there'd been no new graffiti, she wanted to check the footage to be sure no one had been skulking around the building.

She spent the next thirty minutes skipping through eight hours of absolutely nothing. The video ended, and she chucked the phone on her desk in disgust. What a complete waste of time.

A knock sounded at the door.

"Come in," she called.

Andrew entered with his customary grin. He wore khakis and an untucked plaid shirt. His teacher ID hung from a lanyard around his neck.

"Ronnie said you wanted to see me. Something about needing advice."

Victoria shut her eyes and sighed. "You're not the only one telling me to soften my approach with the children. Our helpful secretary is getting in on the action."

He closed the door and crossed to sit on one of the chairs facing the desk. "What happened?"

She filled him in on Micah's latest escapade. To give Andrew credit, he tried to suppress his laughter but wasn't entirely successful. A chuckle escaped when Victoria got to the part about the little boy running away.

"Tell me"—her courteous tone dripped with snark—"oh great genius of childhood interaction, what should I have done differently?"

He sucked air through his teeth. "Micah's a hard case, but I'll take a guess. What were the first words you said to him?"

"My first words? I told him to stop eating chocolate at eight in the morning."

"Mmmm-hmmm." He tapped a finger to his lips. "Do you suppose the interaction might've been less inflammatory if you started with kinder words?"

"Kinder words?"

"I'll give you an example. Repeat after me. I'm so glad to see you."

She ground out, "I'm so glad to see you."

"No." He shook his head. "You sound like you're considering a plate of broccoli."

"I happen to enjoy broccoli."

"You know what I mean. It's not convincing. Inject some enthusiasm into your tone."

Victoria lifted both eyebrows and allowed her voice to drift into the upper register. "I'm so *glad* to see you."

He smirked. "Now you sound like a psycho in a horror movie."

She reached to the bun at the back of her neck and tucked in a protruding pin. "This doesn't come naturally."

"Neither does playing the violin. With both, you have to

practice." He scooted his chair closer and laid his arms on the desk. "What about Sophie?"

Andrew might be an expert in communicating with children, but he'd lost her.

"I don't understand the question."

His gentle smile soothed her ruffled feathers. Feathers? Oh dear. What if she really was an old crow?

Andrew leaned in closer. "You connect with Sophie more than any of the other children. Am I right?"

"Yes. So?"

"So, practice your kinder words on her. I guarantee, she'll eat them up. There's not the slightest possibility of her rejecting your efforts, no matter how rudimentary."

Victoria lowered her head to the desk, her palms stretched out. "Why is this so hard? I must be in the special ed category for human emotions."

She felt him grasp her fingers and looked up. The brown eyes that met hers were free from judgment. His warm acceptance comforted her and gave her the courage to consider his advice.

"Okay, teacher. What do I say?"

He smiled. "Repeat after me. I—"

The office door opened, and Ronnie stuck in her head. "Excuse me, Ms. Park. There's a parent on the phone, a Mrs. Rivers. She wants to postpone her meeting with you by fifteen minutes."

"Fine. Please reschedule her." Victoria remembered the large male hand holding hers. What if Ronnie got the wrong idea? Victoria rose slightly from her seat. "Mr. Zimmerman is just showing me a helpful method for interacting with the students."

"Did I ask?" Ronnie snickered as she shut the door.

Victoria's attention returned to Andrew. She smoothed the

hair at her neck. "I hope Ronnie doesn't misunderstand the situation. My to-do list is long enough without having to squelch unfounded gossip. Where were we?"

His eyes twinkled. "I love you."

Victoria tugged her fingers away. She balled them into a fist and pressed them against her chest. They vibrated as her heart tried to drill a hole through her rib cage.

He loved her?

They barely knew each other. Granted, they'd forded rough waters together since her arrival in Sweetheart, but why would he vault past the shallower emotions—straight to the deep end? Love was volatile. Dangerous. Unpredictable.

Was he crazy?

"I—" Her voice squeaked out an octave higher than normal. She cleared her throat and tried again. "I beg your pardon?"

He spoke in what she now recognized as his patient teacher tone. "I'm trying to explain the way you should speak to the children. The next time you're struggling to find the right words with Sophie, use these: I love you."

Her heart slammed on the brakes.

She lowered her hand to her lap. Of course he wasn't in love with her. Why would she jump to such an outlandish conclusion? The recent graffiti scandal had made her edgy.

Victoria raised her chin. "I don't recall any principal in my entire school career telling me they loved me. They were kind but firm." She rubbed at a wrinkle in her skirt. "I prefer a more restrained approach. It doesn't seem proper to be overly emotional with the children."

"It's not about emotion. It's about survival."

Her gaze jerked to his. "Survival?"

"Not everyone has a happy childhood. What if you're the only person in that student's life who tells them they're loved?" Andrew paused. He began to speak but stopped. A muscle in his jaw jumped. "As a teacher, I'm required to watch all kinds of safety videos before the school year starts. Some of them deal with heavy topics."

She picked up a pen and twisted it. "Yes. I reviewed the training when I took this position. It's terrible to imagine what some children go through at home."

"Exactly. The statistics prove there are kids sitting in my classroom who experience verbal, emotional, or physical abuse. And they might never reveal it. I don't know which ones are suffering, but I do know they're out there." He curled his lips in, pressed them together, and swallowed hard. "The only things I can do are pray and help them feel loved while they're in my class."

She gripped the pen tighter. Why was elementary school so much harder than college? One would expect young children to be simple. They were complicated for so many unexpected reasons.

Victoria lowered her gaze. "It's a laudable practice to affirm the children, but—" She hesitated. Would he think her cruel if she admitted her reservations?

"Go ahead." Andrew tapped the desk. "Lay it on me."

She looked him in the eye. "I value honesty. It's the creed I live by. I don't say things I don't mean. I want these children to recognize their worth and feel loved and valued, but I don't want to be phony. If there's one thing I've noticed since being here, it's that the kids are smart. They'll sense if I'm full of it." Victoria held up her palms. "How can I tell them I love them when I can't even remember their names?"

Andrew leaned back and studied her.

She squirmed under his scrutiny. "Am I an insensitive monster?"

The corner of his mouth quirked. "On the contrary, you're

the kind of champion these kids need—not some bleeding heart with good intentions who will leave them at the first sign of inconvenience.”

“Champion?” she scoffed. “I’m much too practical. That’s one of the reasons I find the words *I love you* difficult. I don’t say them unless I mean them.”

“Perfect.” He stood with a grin. “You can start today.”

She rose from the chair with a sigh. “Didn’t you listen to anything I said?”

“I pay attention to every single thing about you.” He cast an admiring glance over her. “Correct me if I’m wrong. Weren’t you the one who declared love was a choice, not an emotion?”

“Yes. The night of the wedding reception.”

“You’ve got a good memory. My point is this: choose to love the students. You don’t have to experience a fluffy wave of affection surging through you. A basic love of humanity is still love.”

His words hit her and tunneled deep inside with the speed of a subway train. She didn’t have to feel warm fuzzies coursing through her veins. People chose to love their families, friends, and spouses even when they got on their nerves.

It was true. Love was a choice.

ANDREW READ THE EMOTIONS FLITTING ACROSS VICTORIA’S FACE.

First, confusion. Followed quickly by realization. Then acceptance. And finally, determination.

She was the most fascinating thing he’d ever seen. How had no man claimed her? He was shocked but thankful they hadn’t.

This zealous woman had acquiesced to his emotional tutoring with the same honest passion she approached any task. He'd like to pick her up and spin her around. Or crazy dance in the parking lot. Or kiss her under the porch light of their duplex.

Whoa!

The last thought gobsmacked him.

Kiss her?

Yes, kiss her. Their brief peck at the reception had hinted at the fire they might stoke together. Such an idea was entirely unprofessional. He was pretty sure that would be Principal Park's reaction if he ever tried.

But Andrew didn't want to kiss Principal Park. He wanted to kiss Victoria.

Who was he kidding? He wanted to kiss Principal Park too.

Every single incarnation of this woman entranced him, including when she was bossy and annoying. He'd realized long ago, he found her attractive. Today, the emotions he felt ran deeper. How much deeper, he wasn't sure. But one thing was certain. He wanted more. Now that he'd admitted it to himself, how did he go about telling her?

"I like you," he blurted out.

Andrew froze. Talk about unrehearsed. He was as gauche as a twelve-year-old boy asking his crush to the school dance. How would the sophisticated New Yorker react? Laugh in his face?

Victoria's face remained calm. "I like you."

"Huh?" His eyes widened.

Her head tilted to the side. "Aren't we practicing what I should say to the kids?"

His heart, along with his ego, deflated like a balloon with a hole in it. She believed his awkward confession was part of the tutoring. But that didn't change the fact he'd meant every word.

Decision time.

Play it off or go for broke?

Victoria checked her watch. "Will the lesson be over soon? I have a ton of paperwork to complete. The school board called a special meeting and agreed to the cameras, but first, they want a detailed report with research on the latest models and comparative prices." She looked at Andrew. "Was there anything else?"

He manufactured a smile. "Nope. Good job."

"Thanks for the tutoring. Maybe I can practice on Sophie at dismissal. If I work up the nerve."

"Don't be too hard on yourself. Being vulnerable is difficult for all of us."

He left the office and closed the door. The gentle click sounded so final. He expelled a breath and pumped his arms. What was the old cliché?

Patience is a virtue.

So why did it feel like he'd blown it big time?

Chapter Twenty-Five

"Correct." Victoria held the phone to her ear. She kept an easy pace as she walked through the school. Her right foot wasn't crazy about being in a regular shoe. The extra-stiff sole reminded her not to bend her healing toe too much. "There was nothing on the video, Katherine. Just an endless cycle of lizards and bugs." She paused. "But I'll set it up again. I doubt the vandal has rehabilitated."

Someone bumped her.

"Oh, excuse me!" Ms. Amy covered her mouth with both hands. "I'm sorry. We're late for the presentation."

Victoria waved her on.

Ms. Amy and the art teacher hurried past and disappeared inside the gym doors at the end of the hallway.

Screams echoed from inside.

Victoria froze. "Katherine, I'll call you back."

She hurried to the gymnasium entrance and wrenched open the right door. Inside, children sat in semi orderly rows. A woman in a khaki outfit and safari hat stood at the front with a large, yellow python wrapped around her neck.

Victoria's heartbeat returned to a normal tempo. She'd

forgotten about the animal exhibition scheduled for two o'clock. Backpacks lined the gym walls. Classes would leave straight from the presentation to dismissal. The looks on the enraptured children's faces told her they loved their special visitors.

"Don't be scared." The demonstrator uncurled the snake's pliable body and held it out. "Annabelle's as gentle as a kitten. She sheds less too. Do I have a volunteer to hold her?"

Hands shot in the air. A little boy with a shaved head was chosen from the second row. His eyes rounded as the supple python was laid across his shoulders. Classmates squealed and wiggled in awe. He basked in all the attention until the woman retrieved her reptile friend and sent the child back to his seat.

Safari Lady returned Annabelle to her container, then pulled a large box from under the table and opened the lid. "I have another special friend in here. What do you suppose it is?"

The students called out answers.

"A cat!"

"A fish!"

"A dinosaur!"

She lifted out a hard, brownish ball. "This is Aggie the armadillo. She's a mammal, and this hard shell protects her. When she gets nervous, she curl ups and hides. Is there a teacher who'd be extra nice to Aggie?"

"Let Mr. Z!" called Micah from the front row.

"Mr. Z! Mr. Z!" The children chanted.

Andrew jogged down the side and joined the lady at the front. He held his hands clasped over his head like a prizefighter. The students cheered.

Victoria tried to contain her smile. Maybe the reason Andrew Zimmerman related well to the children was because he was just a big kid himself. He bounced on his heels as the animal lady passed him the armadillo.

She pointed out a few salient facts as Andrew walked around the gym, giving the kids in the back a closer look. When the instructor moved on to a pair of tarantulas, Andrew joined Victoria near the door.

He offered the coconut-shaped ball in his hand. Victoria made out a pair of beady, black eyes staring from the hole. The armadillo curled tighter.

"I don't think it fancies me," she said.

"Don't know why." Andrew raised it close to her nose. "You two have a lot in common."

"I beg your pardon?" Her right eyebrow lifted of its own accord.

"You both have a hard outer shell that's difficult to penetrate." He grinned. "And you're softer on the inside than people suspect."

The tips of her ears burned. A rat in body armor. Was that a step up or down from a crow? Neither description was the worst thing she'd ever been called. Her insecure ex-boss had said worse many times when he thought Victoria wasn't listening. She should have worked harder to win him over. He must have been one of the people who campaigned to fire her.

"You okay?" Andrew stroked the tiny mammal with his lean fingers. It uncurled a bit and wrapped around the palm of his hand.

"Are you talking to me or Aggie?"

"Both. Since you two are so symbiotic."

Victoria pressed her lips together. "At least you didn't compare me to the snake."

He laughed and returned to the display, where he handed the armadillo to the instructor. She started putting everything away as the dismissal bell rang. Teachers scrambled to hurry their students, grab backpacks, and tie errant shoelaces.

Victoria picked up Sophie from Mrs. Dole and gave the little girl a few minutes to climb on the jungle gym behind the school before they made their way out front to the usual bench.

Sophie played in the dirt at her feet while Victoria typed on her phone. Katherine had emailed her new information for the report the school board requested. If Victoria worked late, she could send the research to their inboxes by morning.

Were there any other texts?

Leaving her phone in her office at night was not the handiest plan. But she needed to keep the graffiti wall under surveillance. If the vandal struck again, she'd have video proof.

A gentle sigh from Sophie distracted her. The child sat on the curb and picked a small, purple blossom growing from a crack in the sidewalk. She held the flower close to her nose and stared cross-eyed at it. After hopping up, the little girl offered it to her without a word.

"Oh." Victoria put her phone away and took the tiny gift. "Thank you, Sophie."

"Welcome." She looked toward the parking lot.

"Don't worry. I'm sure your mother will be here soon."

"Yeah." She crouched next to her backpack on the ground and tugged at the strap. "My mom's busy. She works hard."

"Yes, she does." Victoria reached out and patted the little girl's arm. "It's because she loves you and wants to give you a good home."

"Uh-huh." Sophie kicked the bag.

"Just the ladies I wanted to see." A cheerful baritone sounded behind them.

"Mr. Z!" An instant smile appeared on Sophie's face. She ran around the bench and hugged him.

He tugged on a springy, black curl and led her to sit by Victoria. Andrew sat on the other side. "How did you like the animal lesson?"

"It was awesome." Sophie kicked her feet, her attention glued to the man beside her.

The slightest ping of jealousy hit Victoria. Andrew was the permanent favorite of all the children. Even if she worked for years, she might never supplant him.

What a futile thought. She didn't have years. A few more months, and Sweetheart would be a charming speck in her rearview mirror.

Beep. Beep.

Sophie threw her arms around Andrew. "Bye, Mr. Z!"

Victoria stood and placed a hand on the child's back. "Let's go, sweetie."

They walked together to the curb. Mrs. Harris pulled her car to a stop, and Victoria opened the passenger door.

"See you tomorrow. And, Sophie?" Victoria hesitated. Perhaps it wasn't the right time with Sophie's mother in the car. Would it sound strange to Mrs. Harris? Too personal?

She cast a glance at Andrew. He waved his chin at her, prodding her on. *Just say it!* She heard his voice inside her head.

Victoria faced the waiting girl. "I-I love you."

"I love you too," Sophie said.

No inhibition. No awkwardness. She didn't even turn around as she climbed onto the front seat.

Mrs. Harris gave a grateful smile and focused her attention on getting her daughter's seat belt fastened. Nothing was mentioned about Victoria's three little words. Was it really this easy to say the phrase she'd agonized over?

She shut the door, a little stunned. It must be a Southern thing. Or maybe a Texas thing. Did everyone go around saying, "Bye now. I love you"?

She returned to the bench and sank beside Andrew.

He raised two thumbs. "Nice work, my star pupil. You get an A plus."

"Sophie didn't even blink." Victoria stared at the departing car. "Like she wasn't surprised."

"She wasn't." Andrew stretched his hands above his head. "Children are perceptive. You may believe that was the first time you told Sophie you loved her, but you've been doing it for weeks now. Every time you gave her your undivided attention. Every time you let her run around on the playground while you waited. Every time you sat quietly beside her or read her a story." He poked her shoe with the toe of his sneaker. "You were saying, 'I love you,' and didn't even know it. But Sophie did."

She motioned on each side of her head like her brain was exploding. "No wonder you get frustrated with me."

He puckered his mouth and looked up. "Mmmmm. *Frustrated* isn't the word."

The dubious twist of her lips made him laugh.

"Okay. *Frustrated* might be the word sometimes. But it's more than that. You're technically my boss."

"Technically?"

"I met you at the wedding before you worked here, so I feel our relationship belongs in a more personal category."

"Relationship?" She should stop this conversation, but she wanted to hear what he would say next.

He scratched his jaw, where a five-o'clock shadow was starting to form. "The truth is, I don't think of you as a boss. Never have."

Her molars clenched, and her internal temperature simmered. Did he have to state in plain English how much he didn't respect her? It was obvious. No verbal slap down necessary.

"Mr. Zimmerman." She held up one finger. "Please don't spell it out. I get it. You refuse to acknowledge me as your superior. Message received."

His entire hand wrapped around her finger. "You need to recalibrate your receiver. That's not the message I sent."

She tried to draw away, but he held tight.

"I don't see you as Ms. Park. I see you as Victoria—the smart, beautiful, confident lady who danced the best Running Man I've ever seen. You make me nuts with your changes and improvements and dress codes, but those are all part of the thing I admire the most about you. Your commitment. You could never be the kind of person who ignores a problem, especially when it involves the children."

She ran her free hand over her slicked-back hairstyle and turned her face away. "It's my job. I'm the principal—"

"I respect your position and abilities, but to me, you're not the principal. You're a woman. A beautiful woman. A woman I'd like to kiss for the second time, only better."

Better?

Her head snapped his direction. Victoria's toes—the ones that weren't broken—curled in her shoes.

Their first kiss was brief yet memorable, an unexpected shock of static electricity.

Andrew's eyes squinted as if his brain had just processed the words that flew from his mouth. He took in a lungful of air. "Oops. I didn't mean to admit so much." He released her finger. "It's true, but I'm afraid it's a bit soon. I should've saved it for the second date."

"Did I miss the first?" Her head cocked.

He stood and propped his hands on his hips. "Not officially. But we've slow-danced, shared a kiss, eaten meatloaf, and played a duet. I've even wiped your runny nose. Surely all of that adds up to the equivalent of one date."

As much as she'd like to experience Andrew's definition of *better*, logic overrode her more feminine instincts. Sweetheart was a temporary aberration from her well-ordered life, a detour from her five-year plan. If she ever took the off-roading adventure Andrew Zimmerman offered, Victoria might never find her way back to the course she'd set for herself.

But he was right about one thing. They'd shared many unexpected moments since she moved here. He was the main reason life in Sweetheart was bearable, and she didn't want to hurt him.

As her brain frantically replayed their current conversation, she realized he hadn't actually asked her out or made a move to kiss her. He'd merely stated a desire to do so. Out-and-out rejection could be avoided unless he left her no other recourse.

Victoria stood. "I have a report to finish. Thanks for your help today." She began to walk away, but his hand at her elbow stopped her.

"One question." He came up behind her.

She swallowed and turned. "What is it?"

His irresistible grin appeared. "What's your favorite kind of pie?"

"My"—that wasn't the question she'd prepared herself for —"my what?"

"Your favorite pie. What is it?"

"Apple." She looked at the hand on her elbow. "Why?"

Andrew released her and stepped back. "I want to make sure I bring the right thing the next time I come calling." His cheery whistle filled the air as he walked away.

Victoria made a right hook motion at his head. Flirtatious jerk. Was he serious or messing with her?

Either way, she didn't like it.

Chapter Twenty-Six

A Monday morning mist stretched across the school lawn as Andrew drove into the parking lot. He congratulated himself for arriving early, even skipping his usual daily sustenance from Heavenly Roasters. Plenty of time to sort the bulk bags of heart-shaped sunglasses he'd ordered for the Candy Hearts Festival.

Another car already sat in a space near the front, taillights on. Of course he hadn't beaten Victoria. When did the woman sleep?

He drove into the spot to the left of her sedan. It shuddered as she killed the engine. Andrew took his teacher ID from the cup holder and slipped the lanyard around his neck. They both climbed from their cars. He grimaced at her over the roof.

"Sounds like your loaner is on its last legs. We should carpool. It saves money on gas and helps the environment."

"No thanks." She slammed her door. "You don't want to be stuck here until seven o'clock or later each night."

A delightful aroma tickled his nose. He noted with envy the steaming cup of fresh coffee in her hand. She must have gotten up with Old Blue. He hadn't even heard the pesky rooster.

As Victoria made her way to the building, Andrew walked backwards beside her. "At least consider clocking out earlier. Anything you're working on will still be here in the morning."

She kept her eyes trained ahead. "I appreciate your advice, however—"

He waited for her comeback, but it never materialized.

She halted. Stared at something.

Andrew looked behind him and flinched. A new crow painting decorated the front wall. This one was the worst yet. The feathered head remained the same, but the torso had been plucked as bare as a Thanksgiving turkey, with only a few springy feathers sticking from the tail. Its scrawny bird legs knocked together at the knees. A red splotch smeared the stomach. Had the painter hurried?

Victoria raced forward, only the slightest of limps visible now that she was wearing regular shoes. Andrew followed close behind. They stopped in front of the graffiti and read the new speech bubble at the top.

It said, "Maintain a high standard!"

Andrew turned to block the image with his body. He searched his brain for the right words. This must be a gut punch to Victoria's pride.

She prodded him aside. Her eyes scanned the unflattering painting. She fingered the red splotch, and a triumphant smile lit her face. "The perp's getting sloppy." She nodded and marched to the building. "Excellent."

Excellent? He'd drop this picture in the *perfectly awful* category. What was he missing?

Andrew scrambled to catch up with Victoria, who'd already unlocked the front doors.

"Is there something I don't know?" He walked with Victoria to her office. "Did you develop a sudden fondness for the defacement of school property?"

"Don't be ridiculous." She crossed to the window where her cell sat atop a stack of books. Victoria grabbed the phone and waved it. "I'm happy, because we can finally catch this miscreant." She tapped the screen and swiped several times.

"We got him!" Victoria threw her arms around Andrew's neck and laughed.

He joined her though he wasn't sure what they were celebrating. She wiggled with glee and released him. The cold rush of air when she moved away chilled his heart.

She pumped her fist. "I left my phone filming overnight from my office window. After two separate graffiti incidents, the vandal was sure to strike again. This time, I've got him on camera."

He stuck his tongue in his cheek. "You never cease to amaze me."

"I'll take that as a compliment." She dropped onto a seat in front of her desk.

He perched on the arm of the chair and peered over her shoulder. "It was meant as one. Do you recognize the guy?"

Victoria unlocked her phone. "I got so excited when I saw someone enter the frame, I stopped watching." She pulled up the video and hit Play.

They observed a figure in baggy jeans and an oversize sweatshirt arrive on the right of the screen. The hoodie's strings were drawn tight to obscure the person's face. Black gloves covered their hands, and ski goggles blocked their eyes. They stalked with a large duffel bag to the wall. The security lights on the school lit the painter's form but gave no clue to their identity.

It took surprisingly little time for the vandal to create the new painting. The hooded figure finished the last flourish on the crow's spiny tail, looked straight at the camera, and gave a two-fingered salute to their forehead.

"Wow." Andrew leaned back. "Is it possible he knew you were filming?"

"Or she," Victoria murmured. "You can't tell anything except for their height. I'd guess five foot three or four."

He nodded. "That does point more toward a woman. But it could be a shorter male or a teenager out making trouble."

Victoria dropped the phone on her desk. "There must be a way to catch this guy." She pressed her fingers to her temples. "Or girl." She huffed. "Kid. Whoever!"

Andrew rose and ruffled his honey-brown hair. "It appears the culprit enjoys taunting you. This is personal. Do you have any enemies?"

She side-eyed him. "Are you kidding?"

"I'm not talking about people you've annoyed. I admit, that list would be lengthy."

She stiffened and went to sit behind her desk. Picking up a pen and paper, she glared. "If you'll excuse me, Mr. Zimmerman, I need to catalogue my enemies. You won't want to wait since it's sure to take most of the day."

"Sorry." He propped his hands on the desk. "I didn't mean to hurt your feelings. It's not a bad idea to think about who might be doing this to get under your skin. I'm going to find the paint bucket and cover the new graffiti before anyone gets here. It'll just be you and me who sees the culprit's work."

Victoria tapped her forehead with the pen. "Just you and me? Not a bad idea." She stood. "I'll help. If we cover this miscreant's handiwork before they get a chance to show it off, it should make them furious." She headed for the door.

How did a woman with a still-mending broken toe move so fast?

Andrew scrambled to keep up with her. "And why is provoking the vandal a good thing?"

They exited the office and turned toward the custodian's supply closet. Victoria set a quick pace, but he stayed on her heels. Her head tilted forward like a football player about to plow into a scrimmage.

"If we make the painter mad enough, they might strike tonight." She spun round, and he bumped into her.

Andrew steadied them both. "Are you hoping to catch them on camera?"

"No." She smiled. "I'm hoping to catch them in person." Victoria pulled away and started walking. "Let's get the paint."

"Wait a minute!" He followed her. "That's a terrible idea. What if this person is dangerous? You shouldn't confront them alone."

"I won't be alone. The kind mayor of Sweetheart has offered assistance."

"Katherine?" He laughed. "As scary as she can be, I'm worried the two of you will end up with more than you bargained for."

"She's already been through this." Victoria swatted her hand. "Katherine told me all about how she caught someone who was burning posters or something at night."

They reached the closet, and Andrew opened the door.

"Yes, I heard the story. It was her and Ryan." He raised a finger. "I repeat. Ryan. At the risk of sounding chauvinistic, it might help to have a male presence nearby. If you insist on spending the night at the school, at least let me come along for safety's sake."

"I don't know. If Mrs. Biddle found out, her tongue would wag a hundred miles a minute."

He grinned. "Katherine can be our chaperone. What do you say?"

She gave a slight quirk of her chin. "It's feasible. Less

chance the person will get away if it's three to one. Okay. You're invited."

Victoria grabbed the paint can. She checked inside and grimaced. "It's almost gone. I hope there's enough to cover the graffiti. Let's get to work."

Chapter Twenty-Seven

Victoria sat on her knees and leaned against the back cushions. The ancient, floral couch creaked underneath. Her elbows rested on the sill as she stared out the window of her darkened office. Two in the morning, and no sign of the vandal.

At her side, Katherine kept determined eyes pointed at the murky darkness. She munched her third chocolate chip cookie while they waited. And waited.

Andrew relaxed on the office floor, body stretched atop a sleeping bag, complete with inflatable camping pillow. His hands were folded over his chest, and the rhythmic rise and fall indicated he was asleep.

Victoria surveyed the peaceful music teacher. "He came to protect us."

Katherine gave a soft laugh. "If Ryan hadn't gone out of town for a seminar, I imagine he'd be here too. He'll be hopping mad when he finds out. I plan to blame everything on you."

"Blame away." Victoria grasped a pair of bright-green

binoculars she'd borrowed from a first-grade teacher. She adjusted the rubber eyepieces and lifted them to her face. "He won't have much to say when we tell him we caught the culprit."

"Right." Katherine thumped her fist on the windowsill. "It's time we stop this loser." She extended the cookie package. "Want one?"

"No, thanks."

Katherine slipped another cookie out and nibbled. Victoria shook her head. Her sister-in-law had a sweet tooth the size of a skyscraper.

They shared the binoculars as they waited. Nothing broke the stillness outside. The security light near the front door gave an occasional flicker, and the wind howled in low, mournful gusts.

Katherine shivered. "I went to school here when I was a kid, but I didn't know how creepy it gets at night."

A wailing whoosh punctuated her statement by rattling the bushes.

Yawning sounded behind them. Andrew stretched in his sleep and flopped on his side. They exchanged amused glances.

Katherine brushed at the cookie crumbs on her shirtsleeve. "Ryan would insist on coming if we'd bothered to tell him. He's my husband and your brother. But why is the music teacher here?"

Victoria twisted the focus on the binoculars. "He wants to catch the vandal."

"Uh-huh." Katherine motioned the length of the sleeping bag. "He's burning with passion."

"I'll set an alarm in case we nod off too."

Victoria typed the instructions on her smartwatch. She checked the cell phone propped against the window to make sure it was recording. It didn't hurt to have video proof to support their eyewitness accounts.

Her sister-in-law rubbed her stomach. "Still hate me for making you move to Sweetheart?"

"What?"—Victoria blinked—"I never hated you. Not really. I just, I didn't—"

"Couldn't stand me, right?" Katherine chuckled. "Don't worry. I won't take it personally. I know my, shall we say, aggressive personality tends to create a bad first impression."

Victoria hadn't realized her sister-in-law was so self-aware.

"I like you now," Victoria offered.

"That's good. Because I plan to stick around the Park family for quite a while."

"I'm sure Ryan would be glad to hear it."

They shared a smile, a sweet moment of harmony, until the eye contact lasted too long, and it got awkward. In unison, they turned to the window.

After a few minutes, Katherine's breath hissed through her teeth. She sank on the couch and gripped her belly. "Maybe I shouldn't have eaten so many cookies."

"Maybe?"

Katherine climbed off the couch. Her body hunched over. "I need to visit the restroom. Are you good on your own?"

"No problem." Victoria waved her away. "Take your time."

She raised the kiddie binoculars then scanned the perimeter of the school grounds. Not a hint of movement.

The couch springs squeaked beside her.

"That was quick," she said.

"What was quick?" a masculine voice asked.

She jerked and found Andrew. He gazed back with sleep-glazed eyes, hair stuck up at the nape of his neck.

He tapped the binoculars in her hand. "Do those things even work?"

"Not well." Victoria gestured to the door. "Katherine's in the restroom."

He yawned and rubbed both hands over his face. "I'll try to behave myself till the chaperone returns."

His tall frame filled the space, and the office seemed to shrink. In the quiet darkness, his soft breaths reverberated.

Victoria drummed her fingers. Where was Katherine? Perhaps it would be less uncomfortable if Andrew and Victoria talked about something while they waited.

"Have you ever played your cello for the students?"

His relaxed form grew tight. He made an almost imperceptible shift away. "No."

"Why not?"

A pause ensued before he answered. "Children love to ask questions. I'd hate for them to discover their music teacher is a washed-up musician."

"I'd hardly call second chair with a respected symphony orchestra *washed up*. And consider how much good you're doing in your current job. All the kids adore you."

"It doesn't change the fact I gave up on my dream," he murmured.

The obvious response was to correct Andrew. Make him understand how valuable he was. But a part of her related to his disappointment. The bitter taste of failure haunted her every morning she walked the halls of an elementary school instead of a venerable university.

It was so very far from where she'd planned to be.

Victoria observed his profile. Strong jaw. Slight crease in his cheek where his hidden dimple sometimes appeared.

She spoke in a somber tone. "Funny thing about dreams. Sometimes they bring more pain than pleasure."

He didn't look at her, which made it easier to continue.

"That doesn't mean we can't start over. Dream again."

Andrew squinted and drew closer to the glass. "Did something move?"

"Hmmm?" She focused on the dark yard. "Where?"

He pointed to the far corner of the parking lot.

A figure came into view. Skulking along in the same hoodie. Duffel bag under their arm. They approached the wall, dropped their stuff on the ground, and crouched.

"Let's get him." Victoria vaulted from the couch and sprinted for the door. She ran from the office, down the hallway, and around the corner. The main entrance was close. She'd be on the culprit in less than a minute. Tiny jolts of pain shot through her not-quite-mended toe, but she pressed on.

Andrew raced past her. He reached the double glass doors and paused.

"Go on," she called. "Don't wait for me."

His conflicted gaze dropped to her foot and returned to her face. His lips firmed, and he exited.

Victoria hurried to catch up.

As she left the building, the painter spotted them, dropped a spray can, and bolted. Andrew gave chase.

Victoria picked up speed. She passed the graffiti wall, and her foot caught on the strap of the discarded duffel bag. She launched forward. Her palms scraped the sidewalk. She landed in an inglorious heap.

Andrew was at her side in an instant. "Are you hurt?"

"Forget me!" She pointed at the figure disappearing in the distance. "Don't let him get away."

He hesitated a millisecond and took off.

Victoria lifted her hands and moaned. Long, angry scratches covered them. She curled to a sitting position and rotated different body parts, making sure she hadn't broken anything else.

But a few bruises were a small price to pay for apprehending the reprobate defacing their campus. Andrew probably had the culprit in custody already. Once they unmasked the scoundrel, she'd call the police.

Chapter Twenty-Eight

ndrew rushed to the chain-link fence surrounding the school property. The gate stood open, and he sprinted through. A section of oak and pine trees stretched along the property line—the perfect place to make a getaway.

He ran deeper into the woods. Streetlamp glow faded. Spiny branches slapped him in the darkness. He stopped and hunched over, stilling his breath, hands propped on his knees.

No crunching leaves. No crashing branches. Nothing.

Had he taken the wrong direction? Or was the culprit lurking somewhere behind a tree? How would Andrew explain if he lost the vandal?

He spent ten minutes examining every spot someone might be hiding. Again, nothing. Andrew snatched a pine cone and chucked it. If only he could head home instead of seeing the disappointment on Victoria's face. Disappointment in him.

He'd let her down.

But she'd been sprawled on the ground when he last saw her. He had to make sure she was okay. Andrew returned to the school and found Victoria going through the duffel bag that the vandal abandoned.

She jumped to her feet at his approach. "What happened?" Victoria looked behind him as if she expected to see the runaway in handcuffs.

He gritted his teeth. *Just admit it.* "He got away. It's my fault. I lost him in the woods behind the school. There are no lights back there, and—"

She lowered to the ground and dug in the bag—ignoring his excuses.

Did she blame him?

He drew nearer. "Find anything?"

"Nothing definitive." Victoria sorted through the items. "Spray cans, brushes, cloths. No labels with the words Property of So-and-So." She sighed and stood with the duffel clutched in her hand.

"Let me carry that." Andrew took the handles from her. "You suffered a nasty spill. Are you okay?"

She held up both hands and revealed long, red scratches. "I earned my battle scars tonight."

The sight of the ragged scrapes twisted his gut. He rubbed the back of his neck. "I should've caught the jerk. I'm sorry."

Once more she didn't respond. She must resent him. And why not? He was the one who let the creep escape.

He noted a pronounced limp in her step now that the adrenaline rush was over. They walked to the school and entered the front doors, then stopped at the nurse's office. Victoria washed her hands while Andrew searched the supplies.

He passed her a small packet of salve. "Need any help?"

"I can handle it."

She squeezed the gel onto her palms and rubbed it into the

cuts. Andrew hovered at her side and passed her bandages. She placed the large adhesive pads over each wound.

"I had no idea being an elementary principal was so dangerous."

"All for nothing." He crossed his arms tight. "Sorry I let him get away."

"Nonsense. It was my fault for falling." Victoria tossed the salve packet in the trash can. "You turned back to check on me."

Sweet of her to give him an out. But the truth was undeniable. He'd failed again.

THE TINY NURSE'S OFFICE LEFT LITTLE ROOM FOR MOVEMENT. Victoria felt the frustration roiling off of Andrew. She appreciated his commitment. At least there was one other person at Sweetheart Elementary who didn't see the graffiti as a big joke.

Even with two of them, they hadn't been able to catch the vandal. Wait. Three of them. Why had their cookie-loving compatriot disappeared at the crucial moment?

She peered into the hallway. "I wonder where Katherine is. My enthusiastic sister-in-law is going to be mad she missed the excitement."

"Serves her right. Taking a bathroom break when she's supposed to be on guard duty. Your phone was recording. Right? Maybe it holds another clue."

"Maybe."

Victoria didn't rush to her office to check the video. What was the point? It would show the same thing as last time. An indistinguishable figure escaping.

The futility of the situation overwhelmed her.

"I can't believe we almost had him." She slapped the sink counter and winced. Her scraped palm protested as unwelcome tears threatened to appear, but she swallowed them down. "If I hadn't tripped, you'd have caught the guy."

"It probably put the fear of God in that idiot. Perhaps tonight will discourage any future attempts."

"And if it doesn't?" She hated the defeated tone in her voice.

"Then we won't stop until he's brought to justice. Your sister-in-law is the mayor. Katherine can arrange to put his head in the stocks on Main Street or something."

Victoria laughed. "Promise?"

He gently took her hand in his large one, uncurled her pinky, and hooked it with his own. "I promise."

She focused on their linked fingers. This must be why the kids loved him. Who knew a silly, childish pinky swear could comfort her?

"What?" She glanced up. "You're not going to seal it with a kiss."

Andrew's easy smile faded. "Just waiting for you to ask."

He tilted his head, leaned in, and placed a soft, feather-light peck on her lips. The brief contact seared her.

She wrenched her hand from his. "I—" She stumbled away. "That wasn't what I meant."

He clamped his lower lip between his teeth. "I know. My timing is terrible. If I'd caught the vandal, you'd feel a lot more affection for me."

"I told you. I don't blame you." How many times did she have to say it? "However, the school isn't the proper environment for …" Her voice refused to say the words.

Andrew shoved his hands in his pockets. "Too late to take it back. I'm surprised I held out this long. I've tried to keep my distance, but you're too irresistible."

"Irresistible?" The description horrified the professional part of her. But the woman inside squealed like a high schooler finding a love note in her locker.

"Might as well go for broke." Andrew squared his shoulders. "If there's one lesson I always try to teach the kids, it's to be honest. So, I'll be straight with you. I've wanted to kiss you for quite a while. Pretty much, starting the moment after the first time I kissed you."

Victoria's gaze jerked to the door. Would Katherine come walking in? She didn't want anyone else hearing his confession.

She didn't want to hear his confession.

It confused her. Overwhelmed her. And knocked on the dusty box where she'd locked her heart, along with any dreams of love and family.

He gave her an opportunity to respond, but Victoria remained quiet.

"I realize this breeches the business-only barrier you insist on maintaining. But we met before we were colleagues. Isn't there some sort of grandfather clause that allows a romantic relationship between us?"

"Romantic?"

One-word answers were all she mustered as the red-hot reminder of his kiss lingered on her lips.

Andrew retreated the length of a ruler. "I want to make it clear, I'm moving in the opposite direction than I'd prefer. But I'm trying to give you space. To process. Or fume. Or whatever." He studied her. "If you decide a more personal relationship between us is feasible, tell me. I'd be happy to seal your decision with something better."

"Better?"

That word again!

From the way her cheeks radiated, she wasn't sure she could handle a high-quality kiss. The miniscule peck he'd placed on her lips was in danger of melting her right down to her fractured toe.

Victoria cleared her throat. "I understand."

Two words. What a breakthrough!

Andrew's eyes lacked their usual sparkle. His declaration had been tinged with sadness, as if bracing for a rejection.

And he wasn't wrong.

She hugged her arms to her stomach. "I'm sorry, Andrew. I'm not sure what to say. If we didn't live in two different states, my answer might be different. But my plans in Sweetheart are temporary."

"Plans change." He stepped forward. "I wanted to kick myself after the wedding. I'd never met a woman I'd felt such a strong connection with, and I let you walk away." He took another step until the tips of his shoes almost touched hers. "It was like God offered me another chance. I don't want to give up so easy this time."

Everything from her scraped palms to her corpuscles tingled. How was she supposed to remain aloof when a sweet, kind, gorgeous guy with mad cello skills coaxed her? She tilted slightly in his direction.

"Victoria?" Katherine's voice called from the hallway. "Andrew? Where is everyone?"

He pointed at the open doorway. "I'll go fill her in on what she missed."

Victoria managed to stay on her feet until he disappeared from sight, then sank to the padded bench by the wall.

Oh, this was bad.

Her emotions spun like a hyperactive kindergartner. Where was the woman who'd broken up with her college boyfriend, because she wanted more time to study? She didn't recognize this giddy, flustered version of herself.

Forget the work-related issues that made his suggestion a terrible idea. From the way his brief touch shook her to the core, she was in great danger of tossing her dreams of career, success, and big-city life into the nearest trash can. Anything for another kiss.

Chapter Twenty-Nine

Victoria smoothed a brush through her loose hair and checked her reflection in the bedroom mirror. Was a fuzzy pink sweater with gray dress slacks an appropriate look for a weekend festival celebrating love? She preferred jeans but had her professional image to maintain. At a town function, there were sure to be lots of students and their families.

Being the elementary principal in a small town was a lot like being a celebrity. She'd once caught someone filming her with their phone when she'd ventured into the grocery store on a Saturday in sweats and a ball cap. No need to give the parent paparazzi more fodder for their chat rooms.

Where had she left her purse?

She wandered into the living room and heard the soft strains of Andrew's cello through their shared duplex wall. He'd practiced every night this week. Sometimes, she sat on the couch and listened to the beautiful, muted sounds.

Other than required school interactions, they hadn't spoken since their kiss in the nurse's office. Probably because she'd avoided him. Andrew had called her irresistible, and she found him the same. But her inevitable departure from Sweetheart was never far from her thoughts.

Her brain always took precedent over her heart. At least up till now. She wasn't about to chuck a lifetime of logical decisions out the window for a temporary fling.

Victoria spotted her purse on the floor by the door. She grabbed it and left the apartment. After jogging down the front steps, she climbed in her sedan and started the engine.

Or tried to.

It sputtered and coughed like a child taking its medicine. The car shuddered. It jolted forward a few inches and died.

"Oh no." She turned the key in the ignition. A discouraging click-click-click answered. "No, no, no!" She swatted a hand against the peeling leather steering wheel.

A movement past the windshield distracted her.

In jeans and a long-sleeved, gray pullover, Andrew stood at the front of the car. A black jacket draped over his arm, a large, white box in hand. He made a face and hollered. "Doesn't sound good."

Victoria climbed from the sedan and slammed the door. "Do you think it's the battery?"

"No idea." He shrugged. "I know guys are supposed to learn about cars when they grow up, but I spent my time in the band room, not shop class."

She glared at her sister-in-law's junker. "What do I do now?"

"If you're going to the festival, I'll give you a lift." Andrew crossed the driveway to his car and opened the passenger door. "Won't even charge you."

She ran the options through her brain, but his suggestion made the most sense. What harm was there in sharing a ride? A few minutes there and back.

"Thank you." Victoria followed and settled inside.

He put on his jacket, walked around the car, and climbed in. After starting the engine, he gave her a thumbs-up. "You look good."

"Mmmm." She hoped her noncommittal grunt discouraged any more compliments. Or kisses. Or anything.

Because her willpower was ebbing.

The drive ended almost as soon as it began. A notable advantage of living in Sweetheart was that it took less than ten minutes to get anywhere. Victoria must have spent the equivalent of months sitting in big-city traffic. She relished how much time the short commute here saved her every day.

Andrew parallel parked on a side street. They climbed from the car, and he grabbed the white box from the back seat.

"What's in there?" she asked.

He waggled his eyebrows. "You'll have to wait and see."

They walked together toward Sweetheart Memorial Park. The town boasted a mere five thousand residents, and they must have all decided to attend the festival. The exuberant throng filled the park and spilled onto Main Street, where vendors had constructed booths.

Victoria meandered past colorful stands for peppermint hot cocoa, hand-knit afghans, and homemade tamales. The slight chill made it possible to enjoy the evening with just a light sweater. She drew in a breath of brisk air and savored the way it invigorated her insides.

The speakers lining the thoroughfare filled the night with cheerful songs from yesteryear. Victoria smiled as she recognized a girl group from the fifties. "My mom loved this song."

"Me too. Your mom had good taste."

String lights stretched overhead from one side of the street to the other, creating a warm, glowing canopy.

Andrew spread his arms wide. "Aren't you glad you came?"

"I feel like I've stepped onto the set of an old movie musical. Is someone about to tap-dance down the road with an umbrella?"

"Not unless it rains."

A breeze blew through the street and rustled the leaves of the trees, still green in February. New York currently had six inches of snow on the ground. Was Sweetheart a hidden wonderland?

Andrew shrugged out of his jacket. "It's nippy out." He wrapped it around her shoulders and kept walking.

The chivalrous gesture took her by surprise. If he'd offered the jacket, she would have declined. Now that she was ensconced in the cozy cocoon, Victoria really didn't want to give it back.

"Thanks," she murmured.

They explored the booths, drinking hot apple cider and tasting raspberry chipotle salsa on fresh, home-baked bread. Andrew interspersed their snacking with funny stories about his first year in Sweetheart.

At least she wasn't the only one who'd experienced fish-out-of-water syndrome in the charming town. Laughing at his anecdotes, she felt the tension drain from her body. Her comfort level increased along with an annoying suspicion.

This felt like a date.

Was it accidental, or had Andrew behaved that way on purpose?

He pointed at the park. "Almost time for the auction to start. It's the highlight of the Candy Hearts Festival. Our first graders are supposed to sing the state song."

"State song?"

"'Texas, Our Texas.'" He placed a hand to her back, shielding her as a group of noisy teenagers shoved past. "You must have heard it at the school."

"I didn't realize it was an official thing. I'm not sure if New York even has a state song."

"We're pretty proud of this place." He stretched out the arm not holding the white box. "Texas was once its own country. I guess we never fully got over it."

"Maybe that's why I always feel like a foreigner."

They walked down the street and moved toward the rows of folding chairs set up near the decorative, white gazebo. Many seats were already taken by people waiting for the auction to commence. Andrew led them to two empty chairs in the middle.

"This should provide a great view of the fun." He placed his box on the chair to his left.

The second they settled on their seats, a voice trilled from behind.

"Hello, Andrew. Isn't this great?" Belinda slipped into the row, picked up the white box, and sat at his side. She cast a brief glance at Victoria. "Hello, Principal Park." Her attention returned to Andrew.

"Hi, Belinda." He bestowed a friendly smile as he took the box from her. "Did you bring a cake for the auction?"

She cast a forlorn look at Victoria. "I've been so busy with the new regulations at school, I haven't had time for anything else." Belinda poked him with her elbow. "But if I'd known you were interested, I'd have stayed up all night baking."

Victoria observed the woman's obvious efforts as she did everything but try to sit in the middle of them. How shameless was Belinda to shoehorn her way between a couple? Scratch that. Two friends who were enjoying each other's company. Victoria and Andrew were definitely not a couple, though it might appear that way to any normal person.

She angled her body away from the blatant flirting. A man in an old-fashioned tuxedo coat with tails and a black, silk top hat approached the gazebo stage. From the size of his belly, he looked like he knew a thing or two about cake. He climbed the steps to the top and tapped on the microphone. It shrieked, and people in the audience covered their ears.

"Sorry, folks." His deep voice held a distinct Texas twang. "Welcome to the highlight of Sweetheart's annual Candy Hearts Festival, which is the cake auction. I'm your master of ceremonies, Willy Walker."

Cheers and whistles rang out.

"Let's get the party started with a love song about this great state we live in. Will the kids who are performing come on up?"

"That's my cue," Andrew whispered in Victoria's ear.

His breath warmed her chilly earlobe. She was glad he couldn't hear the way her pulse pitter-pattered. She nodded without answering.

He scooted past Belinda to the middle aisle and made his way to the front. The first graders crowded onto the gazebo steps. They wore heart-shaped sunglasses, even though it was nighttime, and stood straight and proud while they sang a cappella. Andrew crouched near the ground and directed them. Parents in the audience raised their phones to video the performance.

When the children finished, a rousing wave of applause swelled. Andrew ducked out the side with his white box and disappeared. Mr. Walker, the auctioneer, returned to his spot as the kids ran to find their parents. He held a large, plastic mallet with a poofy heart on the end.

"Weren't they great?" he boomed. "Give them another hand." The man waited until the clapping faded away. "Now for the fun part. Y'all know how this works. One of Sweetheart's lovely ladies will come on stage with her culinary creation and whoever bids the highest will win a delicious dessert and the pleasure of eating it with the beautiful baker."

Victoria squelched the urge to laugh out loud. How quaint. The women cooked, and the men bid on them. Wouldn't her feminist friends in New York utter a collective scream of horror?

Mr. Walker checked a small index card. "Our first entry is a lady you all love. The belle of Sweetheart, Texas, and quite popular with the menfolk. I expect her cake will go for a pretty penny. Even though she can't cook to save her life."

"Mr. Walker!" A vivacious blonde bounced to his side with a tall cake covered in lemon-colored frosting, which perfectly matched the yellow piping on her vintage navy cardigan and poodle skirt. Victoria recognized her fellow bridesmaid from the wedding.

Willy Walker spoke into the microphone. "Miss Deanna Day, when are you going to quit playing the field and settle down?"

Victoria cringed, but the nosy question didn't seem to bother the lady a bit.

Deanna winked at the audience. "Whenever the right man asks me."

A young man in a cowboy hat hollered from the front row. "I keep asking, but she keeps saying *no*."

Laughter rippled through the crowd.

Mr. Walker leaned out and said in a stage whisper, "Well, son, I suppose that means you're not the right man."

More laughter.

The bidding commenced, and the auctioneer's prediction proved correct. Deanna's cake sold for a whopping one hundred and twelve dollars.

A shy, bucktoothed lad ambled up to claim his prize. Deanna beamed at him. She slipped her arm around his, and they left the stage together. They walked down the middle aisle like it was another wedding. Deanna spotted Victoria in the audience and mouthed a hello.

Victoria waved back as Mr. Walker continued the auction.

"Why, I declare. We have a surprise for the female population of Sweetheart."

Victoria's attention returned to the front, and her shoulders jolted. Andrew stood at the gazebo—a giant pie in his hands. What in the world? Weren't the bakers supposed to be women?

The auctioneer eyed him with pursed lips. "I admit I'm flummoxed. It's not unheard of for a man to enter, but this is a cake auction, son."

"Yes, sir." Andrew's eyes focused on Victoria. "I'm aiming for a certain bidder who prefers pie to cake. Apple is her favorite."

Her breaths shortened. He meant her. She squirmed under the heat of his gaze. The overactive beating in her chest must be disturbing the festival goers. It echoed through her body and pounded in her ears. This good-looking, in-demand town favorite had remembered the one time she mentioned apple pie and baked one to appeal to her.

How embarrassing.

And sweet.

And utterly irresistible.

Click.

The lock on the dusty box where she'd hidden her heart snapped open.

Chapter Thirty

Andrew brandished his pie with a confident smile. No one would suspect he wanted to curl up like an armadillo and roll off the stage. This had to be, without a doubt, the stupidest, most degrading plot he'd ever attempted.

From the look on Victoria's face, she understood the personal meaning behind this apple pie. Her expression was unusual. She looked ... blindsided.

Not the reaction he was hoping for.

Willy Walker hooked a thumb in his silk cummerbund. "You heard him, ladies. Anybody fond of apples?"

At least ten women waved their hands and shouted.

Andrew's smile faltered. His ill-advised plan just went from embarrassing to mortifying. He'd wanted to catch Victoria's attention, but his net had reeled in more fish than he'd bargained for.

Willy leaned over to sniff the pie. "Smells good. And you sprinkled the crust with sugar. The winner won't be disappointed in our music teacher's culinary efforts." He chuckled. "Not that I think it matters."

"Get to the bidding already!" An anxious female voice called.

Andrew flinched, and Willy laughed

"Yes, ma'am." The auctioneer tipped his top hat. "Forgive me for making y'all wait. Can I get an opening bid of ten dollars?"

A chorus of voices answered. "Ten dollars!"

He chuckled. "Let's fast-forward a little. Do I hear fifty dollars?"

Andrew took a bracing breath. This was going to be a long night. But it would all be worth it if a certain beautiful principal stopped avoiding him.

BIDS PINGED AROUND VICTORIA. MULTIPLE WOMEN UPPED THE ANTE at lightning speed. The price skyrocketed for the apple pie and its added benefit of eating with Sweetheart Elementary's most popular teacher.

Andrew waited with a good-natured grin, not repelled in the least by standing there like a bull on the auction block. He tilted the apple pie forward and waggled it at her. She caught Mrs. Biddle giving her a knowing glance from the sidelines.

Victoria's pulse escalated. The town gossip wasn't the only one looking. Heads turned her way from every row. Andrew's culinary declaration made it clear he was interested.

How should she respond?

A bidder on the front row elbowed the woman beside her. "Honey, your hips can't handle another slice of pie. Best leave him to me."

The lady elbowed back, and Willy Walker left the stage to break up the pair.

Victoria's spine straightened. Forget the professional

ramifications. Her pride refused to let her bid on the pie and enter the equivalent of a public catfight.

Belinda Carlyle rushed into the aisle. "Seventy-five dollars!"

Her bid was topped by a woman with teased blonde hair who wore jeans and a tight, pink shirt with a plunging neckline deeper than any Victoria had seen in Sweetheart.

"I have eighty dollars from Renee." The auctioneer waved his gavel in the air, and it knocked against his top hat. "Do I hear eighty-five?"

"One hundred!" Belinda pulled a wad of twenties from her purse.

The aforementioned Renee pushed out of her row and met her in the middle. They faced off nose to nose.

"One hundred fifty," Renee yelled.

"Two hundred!" Belinda shoved her face closer.

This was appalling. Why were these women spending hundreds of dollars on a pie meant for someone else? A fire lit in Victoria's belly. Her toes tapped the dry grass.

Andrew cast a glance her way, his eyes asking, challenging, imploring.

She owed him. He'd done so much for her. Nursing her through the sniffles. Teaching her how to interact with the children. Treating her with kindness when his coworkers kept their distance.

How could she leave the poor man to these female barracuda? It wasn't kosher. They might eat him alive.

Besides, it was *her* pie.

Victoria bent and stretched a hand under her chair for her purse as the blonde woman bellowed at the auctioneer.

"Willy, I'm short on funds! Can I write a check?"

"Sorry, Renee." He crossed his arms. "Cash only. You know that."

Victoria froze mid-reach. Cash only?

What was this town's fascination with paper money? She'd used her credit card from New York to South Korea without a single problem. But Sweetheart refused to accept plastic. Although she'd started carrying a modicum of cash, she didn't have enough to beat the already sky-high bid.

She straightened and looked at Andrew. His brown eyes begged for help. She dropped her gaze and bit the inside of her lip. Guilt flooded.

"Two hundred going once," the auctioneer declared. "Two hundred twice. Sold!" He slammed his gavel on the gazebo railing.

The crowd cheered. People buzzed as Belinda walked to the front.

Andrew met her and passed the pie over with a smile. "I get to eat with a good friend tonight."

Belinda blanched slightly at the description. She took the arm Andrew offered, and they exited to the right. He fetched his white box from a table at the side.

Victoria's heart pounded for a whole different reason. Her toes tapped faster. Somebody slipped alongside, and a familiar burgundy head popped into her field of vision.

"Wasn't that exciting?" Mrs. Biddle squeaked. "I respect a man who's brave enough to stand before the whole town and declare his intentions. But I wish Andrew had said who he meant." Her eyes glinted as she leaned closer. "Do you like apples, dear?"

Victoria answered without a hint of disappointment. "I can take them or leave them. What about you?"

"Me?" Mrs. Biddle tittered. "Oh, they're all right, I guess." The crowd roared, and her attention snapped to the front. "Will you excuse me? I'm missing all the excitement."

"With pleasure."

Victoria sat through the remainder of the auction without paying the slightest bit of attention. Even when an exhibitionist bidder wearing a pair of reindeer antlers appeared and the price reached a thousand dollars, she ignored the rowdy crowd. Her rigid shoulder blades touched the folding chair. The temptation to leave made her heels bounce against the grass. But there were two problems.

First, the busybodies like Mrs. Biddle might misconstrue her exit as being resentful about the pie affair.

And second, Andrew was her ride.

Why had she agreed to carpool on this of all nights?

Talk about a terrible decision.

Her posture loosened as Mr. Walker wrapped up the auction and bid everyone a good night. She took her purse, folded Andrew's jacket over her arm, and stood. It would be awkward to search for him and ask if he was ready to go.

What if his special pie time with Belinda wasn't finished?

Victoria left the auction area and strolled through the park. Her steps were slow, but her eyes were quick. They zipped back and forth in search of the apple pie pair.

"Hey there, little lady." A man with a graying goatee and a leer maneuvered in front of her. "You're new in town, aren't you?"

She recognized him as the clown who'd worn the reindeer antlers to the auction. In February.

Could her night get any worse? What next? A freak snowstorm?

"It depends on what you call new. I've been here almost two months."

His voice lowered as he leaned in. "How did I never happen to hear a pretty young filly moved to Sweetheart?"

Victoria remained impassive. She'd met many a pervert on the subway and found the best response was a calm, measured tone. If that didn't work, a swift kick to the shin usually did the trick.

"I assure you, sir, I'm not a young filly." She bit out the words. "Please let me pass."

Victoria dodged him, but he blocked her way.

"No need to get your dander up. I was paying you a compliment." He smoothed a hand down his goatee. "How 'bout we eat together at The Brunch Café next weekend."

"No, thank you." She stepped to his other side, but he swerved and blocked her again.

Was this some sort of twisted waltz?

"Sorry, John." Andrew appeared to her left. "If Ms. Park ever decides to go out to dinner with anyone, it'll be me. Not you."

The man grunted. "Didn't know there was a prior claim. My mistake." He wandered away.

Victoria spun to glare at Andrew.

"I didn't need any help. And what did he mean by prior claim? I'm not a piece of property you can stick a sign in."

"Agreed." Andrew nodded. "But that's the kind of language a guy like him understands. I was doing you a favor."

"I fight my own battles, thank you."

Did she sound a bit harsh? She must admit his assistance with the stranger's unwelcome advances had been effective. She took a breath.

"I appreciate your good intentions. I'm just"—Victoria pasted a cheerful smile on her stiff lips—"Did you and Belinda finish the pie? Your entry certainly caused a stir. They almost had to call the sheriff."

Andrew cocked his head to one side. His face betrayed no emotion. "You said apple pie was your favorite."

She pressed her lips together, unsure of how to respond. Should she admit she hadn't brought enough cash? It might soften the rejection. He spoke before she found the right words.

"You must have realized I baked it for you. But you didn't even place a bid." He expelled a frustrated puff of air. "Does this have something to do with your all-consuming goal of keeping things professional?"

Why not let him think that? It would end any romantic intentions he had toward her.

"It wouldn't look right if the principal bid on one of her teachers. Especially when the competition is another employee."

"So unprofessional." His tone was sarcastic.

She raised her chin. "I'm sick of being Mrs. Biddle's favorite topic. I want to lie low, do my job to the best of my ability, and return to New York with no regrets."

He stilled. "Are you telling me there's nothing you regret?"

The memory of that night in the nurse's office popped into her mind. Andrew's expression told her his thoughts pointed in the same direction. Heat rose through her body. Their eyes continued the conversation their mouths abandoned.

"There you are!" Belinda bounced to their side, her hard-won dessert in hand. "I'm ready to taste this delicious concoction. Care to join me?"

From the way she batted her lashes at Andrew, it was obvious the invitation didn't include Victoria.

He smiled at Belinda. "You bet. Let me carry it for you." He took the pie from her and looked at Victoria. "I'll text you when I'm ready to leave."

"Why?" Belinda's gaze swerved between them.

Andrew offered her his arm once again. "Since we're neighbors, we carpooled."

There was the briefest pause before she responded. "Oh, I

see." She slid her slim fingers around his biceps. Her eyes sparkled at Victoria. "See you on Monday, Ms. Park."

Victoria managed a dip of her chin. "Enjoy your pie."

The two strolled off, and her teeth scraped together. Perhaps she should have said, "Enjoy *my* pie." It was meant for her, but she'd been too stupid to buy it.

Andrew was right. She did regret something.

Many things.

But at this moment, what she regretted most was not bringing enough cash to the festival.

Chapter Thirty-One

Victoria sat to the left of her brother. The smooth, wooden seat fit her body like a familiar piece of furniture from her own living room. Since her father was a minister, she'd spent a lot of time on a pew.

They'd added a few new songs since the last time she'd attended church, but it didn't put her off. Pastor Thibodeaux's welcoming smile encompassed the whole congregation. He made sure to compliment the musicians before his sermon and give a shout-out to the new trumpet player.

Victoria cast a glance at Andrew sitting across the aisle. His eyes met hers as if he knew what she was thinking. The minister would be complimenting the new cello player if he ever discovered Andrew's ability.

Pastor Thibodeaux's sermon about peace in the storm was tailor-made for Victoria. Had anyone told the pastor she was coming? The Bible verses from the poetic book of Psalms smoothed the wrinkles from her mind.

It felt right. Homey. Good to be back.

Even though this was the first time she'd attended a service in Sweetheart, she felt the same God in this place as she did in her father's church. It was just another branch of the same family.

After the final prayer, Victoria slipped out of the pew and came face to face with Andrew.

His expression was friendly but not in the uninhibited, pre-auction way he used to grin at her. Now his smile was guarded.

He nodded at the pulpit. "You see. I wasn't exaggerating about Pastor Thibodeaux. He loves discovering new talent for the band."

"Don't worry." She leaned forward with a whisper. "Your secret's safe with me."

His lips relaxed the slightest bit into a softer expression. His tall frame towered over her but didn't feel the least bit threatening. He opened his mouth to speak.

Her phone rang. She dug it from her purse. Her heartbeat quickened at the number on the caller ID, but she forced her voice to stay calm. "Pardon me. I have to take this."

Victoria stepped away, wound around the chatting groups, and hit the Answer button when she reached the back doors.

"Hello, Abe." Her tone was breathless, and not because she was hurrying. "It's been a while."

Abe Wilson had been her champion on the university's school board. The one who'd guaranteed her the associate dean position. But he'd been unaware of the political shenanigans in the university's pecking order that gave the job to the son of a board member instead of her.

Victoria exited the church and stood underneath the shade of a tall oak tree. She listened as Abe bemoaned what a mess the new guy made. Vindication swirled inside her. It served the board right for choosing an untried rookie as a favor for their buddy.

"I'm sorry, Abe," she said when he finally ran out of complaints. "It must be terrible. You were always such a stickler for standards and procedures. The new guy must be driving you crazy."

More complaining followed. Abe wound down enough to ask about her new job. She rubbed the scrapes on her somewhat healed hands.

"It's a work in progress. Creating car line flowcharts. Tracking school vandals. Coaxing children to eat a healthy breakfast. You wouldn't recognize me, Abe."

He offered his condolences and made her promise to get together for lunch the next time she was in town. After hanging up, Victoria stared at the phone. Next time? The school year was flying. Only a few months remained before she saw Abe in person.

Melancholy hit, unexpected and unwelcome. The thought of returning to New York should fill her with relief. Katherine had roped her into this temporary principal position against her will. Why didn't she rejoice to be nearing the end?

Mrs. Biddle bustled along the sidewalk with a determined expression. Victoria ducked behind the tree trunk.

In a wheezing voice, the older woman squeaked out, "Good morning, Principal Park. I'm glad I caught you."

Victoria arranged her lips in the closest imitation of a smile she could muster and emerged from her hiding place. "Good morning, Mrs. Biddle. How did you know I was here?"

"I heard your voice when I walked out the front doors." Mrs. Biddle pointed to her left. "Somebody using words like *standards* and *procedures* and *car line flowcharts*? I knew it must be our latest import from New York."

"Did you?" Victoria placed the phone in her purse.

"Yes. Nobody else in Sweetheart talks that way. I raced over to confer with you about something important."

With Mrs. Biddle scuttling by her side, Victoria headed for the parking lot. "Important? Is this about the school?"

"Not exactly. Although I suppose he does work at the school. It's about Andrew Zimmerman."

Victoria picked up the pace. "I'm sorry. Now isn't the best time. Please make an appointment during the week." Her sedan was in sight. She could end this conversation soon. If the disreputable junker didn't refuse to start.

Mrs. Biddle followed her to the car.

"Hi, Ms. Bark!" A young voice hailed Victoria.

Micah stood, holding his older brother's hand near his father's black monster truck.

"Hi, Micah," she called, not bothering to correct him.

The teen glared. "Leave the old crow alone, Micah." He tugged his brother in the opposite direction.

When Victoria turned back to Mrs. Biddle, she found her standing in front of the driver's side door.

Trapped.

Mrs. Biddle smiled. "It won't take long, dear. I've noticed how much you and Andrew enjoy each other's company. I've tried for almost a year to match that boy with someone. He seemed cooperative. Agreed to meet the nice young ladies I wanted to set him up with. But then he always claimed to be busy when I tried to nail down a date. I suspect he had some issues to work through, poor thing. Leaving his big-city symphony job and all."

"You knew about that?"

"It's one secret I've kept to myself. Didn't want to hurt the boy." She flapped both hands. "But my point is this. Once you moved to town, Andrew was practically glued to your hip. He follows you around like a puppy. It really is the cutest thing."

Victoria fingered her key fob. Maybe if she gave a hint, she'd extricate herself from this unpleasant dialogue. She hit the Unlock button. The car beeped.

Mrs. Biddle, overplucked eyebrows raised, continued to

block the door. "I'm not quite finished, but don't you worry. I simply want to advise you to be careful."

Victoria focused. "Careful?"

"Yes. Andrew may look fine on the outside. Always singing, joking, and playing with the kids. But he's wounded somewhere deep. I'm afraid falling for you might make it worse."

The woman's words irritated her. They always irritated her, but this time even more so. What was so wrong with the idea of Andrew and her as a couple?

"Mrs. Biddle, I appreciate your good intentions. Mr. Zimmerman and I can take care of our own relationship without assistance from any outside parties."

"Outside parties? You make it sound as if we need to get the lawyers involved. It may be none of my business—"

"I'd go with that instinct."

Mrs. Biddle snorted. "But you're here for a limited time. Am I wrong?"

The woman wasn't wrong, but why admit it? Pique forced Victoria to keep her mouth shut. Unfortunately, Mrs. Biddle didn't require encouragement and kept talking.

"Let him concentrate on Belinda Carlyle or sweet Amy Kelly. Either one of them would be a much better match." She put her hand with the pointy, purple nails on Victoria's arm. "Think about it, dear. You don't want to hurt him."

Victoria tensed. "I assure you, Mrs. Biddle. I respect Mr. Zimmerman as a valuable employee and a friend. Nothing more. I wouldn't dream of causing dysfunction in the workplace with an ill-advised flirtation."

The unwelcome counselor patted her. "I didn't understand half of what you said, but I got the gist." She snorted again. "Dysfunction in the workplace. Nobody talks like you,

Principal Park, that's for sure. I can hear you coming a mile away."

Victoria forced the corners of her lips up. "And I, you."

She remembered Deanna Day's hasty retreat at the wedding. Now it made perfect sense. The next time Victoria spied Mrs. Biddle, she'd be hightailing it in the opposite direction too. The woman delivered her guidance with all the gravity of a talk show psychiatrist.

Victoria climbed in her car and slammed the door.

Best to erase the unsolicited advice from her mind.

Chapter Thirty-Two

Click. Click. Click. Click.

Victoria's fingers flew over the laptop keys as her brain flew over her weekend run-in with the village gossip. Monday morning, and she was still stewing about their impromptu counseling session. She fanned the neckline of her shirt. Was the thermostat broken, or was it just her internal temperature?

What business was it of Mrs. Biddle's if Andrew Zimmerman baked her an apple pie? Or played a solo concert in her living room? Or flipped her heart inside out with a tender kiss?

The suggestion that Belinda or Amy made more sense as his partner irked Victoria. All the more because it was true. She realized the mountain of obstacles standing in the way of a romantic relationship with the incomparable music teacher. It wasn't necessary for an uninvolved, especially nosy third party to point it out.

Her thumb hit the space bar with extra force. She mocked in a baby tone, "They'd be a much better match."

Her mind replayed their conversation for the umpteenth time. Mrs. Biddle's irritating voice sang out in her head.

"Nobody talks like you Principal Park, that's for sure."

Her fingers pressed the keys in a militant rap. "As if it's a crime to mention flowcharts and standards."

Her hands paused.

"Standards," she muttered.

What words had the last graffiti monstrosity used?

The paintings always mimicked something Victoria said, like in the car line, calling into the megaphone, "Move down, please."

The phrase was one she'd uttered in public around many people. Parents, teachers, staff, and students had heard her. Anyone could have painted it.

But the most recent graffiti said, "Maintain a high standard."

She recalled using that specific phrase on one occasion. It was in the staff meeting when she'd explained the reasons for restricting jeans to casual Fridays. Only people who worked on campus would have heard her.

Victoria retrieved her phone and pulled up the picture she'd taken of the crow with the plucked body. Her eyes zeroed in on the bird's stomach. She pinched the screen and zoomed in. The smear she'd dismissed as a mistake on the painter's part resembled something.

A handprint. A red handprint. Like the one on her skirt the day she subbed for pre-K. She'd worn the outfit in their dress code staff meeting.

Victoria sprang to her feet. She clutched the phone, looking this way and that.

The vandal worked at Sweetheart Elementary.

"Yes!" She fist-pumped in the air. Her shoes scuffed the industrial weave carpet in a celebratory jig.

This was a game changer. It narrowed the possibilities to a select few. Elation subsided as the truth hit. Hard. Someone at school hated her. Really hated her. Enough to slander and subject her to ridicule in front of everyone.

A hard knot rose in her throat. She sank onto the chair and dropped her phone on the desk. Victoria inhaled and exhaled in a measured pattern. No time for tears. She fanned a hand near her face. Her chin firmed. No matter who was behind the vandalism, it must stop. The new information narrowed the suspect pool, but there were plenty of five-foot-four people working at the school. How could she figure it out, short of interrogating every staff member?

A knock sounded at the door. She ran a finger down her desk calendar. Andrew had made an appointment for this time.

"Come in."

He entered with a pair of white gloves in hand. Her lips opened, anxious to reveal her discovery. But should she? If the information was burdensome to her, how much more would it weigh on this amiable man?

Andrew settled on a chair in front of the desk. "Good morning, Principal Park."

She blinked at his formal greeting. "Good morning, Mr. Zimmerman. You wanted to see me?"

"Yes, ma'am." He placed the gloves on her desk and slid them toward her. "The Founder's Day program is this Friday. I've written a special song about Sweetheart and taught it to the second graders with sign language choreography."

Song? Program? She tried to concentrate on his words, but her brain kept zipping back to the recent discovery. If she told him her suspicions, he might be able to offer insight into his coworkers.

Andrew motioned to the gloves. "Would it be possible to

buy a pair of these for every second grader? I already have black lights from a previous performance."

No. She couldn't tell him. It might make him feel like a snitch, and she couldn't place that stigma on him.

"Principal Park?" Andrew's voice beckoned. "Victoria?"

"Hmmm?" She snapped out of it. "I agree. The performance would be cooler with black lights. It's creative. Not something you often find in an elementary school."

"More like a club." Andrew laughed.

She smiled. "I could tell you stories of my younger days, when me and my friends—"

Her gaze jerked to the phone on her desk. She grabbed it and swiped the screen, finding the crow picture.

Andrew leaned forward. "Yes? I'd love to hear about the crazy, young Victoria."

She glanced up at him. "I'm sorry. I'll have to cut our appointment short. Tell Ronnie to print a purchase order for the gloves, and I'll sign it."

Victoria shot from her seat. She'd shortened the suspect list and formulated a plan. All she needed were the right materials.

ANDREW MARKED A DISTRACTED HASTE IN VICTORIA. HER TWITCHY movements communicated an almost frenzy. He caught her as she swerved around the desk.

"Wait a minute. Is something wrong?"

"Something's right." She looked over his shoulder. "I have an idea for catching the person painting the graffiti. Will you help me?"

"Of course." He let her go.

She raised her phone and tapped on the screen. "Can I borrow your black lights?"

Victoria walked off, steps quick and short.

Her request surprised him. Andrew scrambled after her. "When do you need them?"

"Tonight." She swung the door wide.

He caught up and kept pace as she left the office and marched down the hallway. "Tonight? I planned to buy the gloves this afternoon and rehearse with them tomorrow. Will you be done with the lights by then?"

"Yes." She crossed the front entryway and headed along the opposite hall, straight toward the art class. "I'll test my plan after work. If it's successful, I'll borrow them again later. Please follow my lead and don't say anything about what we've discussed. Especially the black lights."

Why the secrecy? Was another all-night stakeout in their future? The memory of the last one and their kiss in the nurse's office warmed his neck. He rubbed the heated flesh and forced his mind back to business.

Victoria barreled through the art room's open door with Andrew close behind.

At her desk, Belinda sat in mid-bite of a sub sandwich. Splotches of purple paint lined the rims of her fingernails. Her eyes widened. She dropped her lunch, grabbed a napkin, and wiped her mouth. "Andrew! What brings you here?" She spared a glance at Victoria. "And Ms. Park."

Victoria motioned to several giant rolls of colored paper on a metal stand. "We're creating a few special posters. Would you mind helping us?"

Belinda left the desk and flitted to Andrew's side. Her skirt with cartoon figures of famous painters on the hem swished as she clasped her hands and rocked back and forth. "I'd love to assist y'all."

Andrew took a tiny step away. Her words included both of them, but her body language indicated him alone. She'd been more aggressive since the pie auction. Would she take a gentle hint, or was it going to require a serious talk?

He slipped a finger under the already unbuttoned collar of his dress shirt and tugged. "What kind of posters, Ms. Park?"

"A few slogans." Victoria crossed to the rolls and chose a light-yellow color. "Such as: Take care of our school. Graffiti is gross. Winners don't write on the wall. I'm sure you've caught my theme."

Belinda's lips pursed. "It's not exactly subtle."

"Oh, one more." Victoria held up an index finger. "Vandals will reap the consequences." She pointed at Belinda. "Will you please work on that one?"

Andrew sat on top of a short table. "Do you think our tiny students will understand the meaning of the word *consequences*?"

"If not, it's time they learned." Victoria returned to the center and faced them, hands on her hips. "I plan to make sure everyone in Sweetheart Elementary grasps the meaning of *consequences*."

Belinda's gaze cut over to him. She rolled her eyes, her mouth rounded in a silent whistle. Andrew couldn't blame his coworker. Victoria's passion for catching the vandal was well-known, but this sounded a bit excessive.

The staff might balk at the principal's hanging incendiary posters around the school. How would they explain them to the young children? Should he say something? Would she recognize his genuine concern or take it as betrayal?

The memory of Sophie and how Victoria accepted the misunderstandings surrounding her tutoring crossed his mind. He'd made the mistake of not trusting Victoria before. And he was wrong. Why not try the opposite tack this time?

Andrew rolled up his sleeves and grabbed an apron from a

hook on the wall. "Let's get to work. I bet I can knock out a couple of these before my break ends."

Belinda looked less than happy. She meandered to her desk. "I'll help as soon as I finish my sandwich. Some of us need nourishment in order to teach."

Andrew grabbed a container of paintbrushes from a shelf on the wall. He wouldn't be eating today. Victoria's grateful smile was reward enough for skipping lunch. But would his sacrifice be in vain?

Chapter Thirty-Three

Victoria passed one of her posters on the way to the gymnasium for the concert. A childish sense of pride swelled at the sight of the silly face with tongue sticking out that she'd painted to accompany the slogan Graffiti is Gross! It didn't fit the Founder's Day theme, but there was a good reason for keeping the posters up.

She entered one of the double doors and scanned the waiting crowd. Rows of orderly chairs faced the stage. At the front, people gathered around the regular principal Mattie Kilgallen, who had delivered her baby early. The new mama beamed and showed off her little girl to one and all. Swaddled in a soft, pink blanket, the preemie slept through all the attention.

Would the woman want her job back early? Probably not. She seemed to be enjoying her maternity leave.

Victoria paced along the folded bleachers. The afternoon rehearsal went off without a hitch. So why was her stomach fluttering like an anxious parent's? Her sense of ownership about Sweetheart Elementary surprised her.

She buttoned her navy-blue suit coat and straightened the

pleats in her skirt. She'd managed to fit into a pair of low dress heels for the occasion. Her mostly mended big toe only protested every once in a while.

Children's artwork lined the gym walls. The paintings depicted Amos Colter, the town's founder, in various western scenes. Sometimes he was a stick figure, and sometimes the renderings actually resembled the statue at the end of Main Street. The program celebrated the day he'd stuck the first fence post in the land that would one day become the town of Sweetheart.

She took a seat on the front row as the lights dimmed. The program went off without a hitch. Micah Crumm played the part of Amos with great aplomb in a flannel shirt, chaps, and fake mustache. Victoria spotted a few people dabbing their eyes during the last song when the second graders presented the sign language with the black-light finale.

Her own self-command crumbled at the tiny, adorable voices extolling the beauties of Sweetheart. What was the matter with her? She wasn't a local. Her jaded New Yorker emotions must be thawing in the warm Texas climate. Not even March, but the last week's temperatures had reached the mid-eighties.

After the show, she approached Andrew, where he talked with Katherine and Ryan.

Her sister-in-law slapped him on the shoulder. "Amazing job, Andrew. Where did you find a song about Sweetheart? It made me weepy."

Victoria slipped into the group. "He wrote it. Composed the music and words himself."

"Wow!" Katherine clapped. "I think we've found our official town song."

Ryan held up his hand. "One question. Will you charge us much to use it?"

Andrew laughed. "I can be persuaded to donate the copyright."

After a few more compliments, the newlyweds excused themselves.

Andrew turned to Victoria. "What's your opinion of the program?"

"I must be getting soft. The line about 'where the hearts are as sweet as its name' kind of got to me." She looked around the gym at the children in their costumes. "I felt proud as a parent when Sophie sang the solo for the kindergarten song."

"Wasn't she great? Would you believe she used to refuse to sing with the group in music class? She's really blossomed."

"Thanks to you."

He waved away the compliment, and she faced him.

"I'm serious. This might not be your dream career of making music with a lauded symphonic orchestra." She pressed her chest. "But the things you're doing with these children have eternal value. Deep down. Who knows how many voices will spend their lives singing because of you?"

Andrew's cheeks reddened. "Wow. I, uh"—he cleared his throat—"I'm not sure what to say. Thank you."

"I meant every word."

He tilted his head. "Perhaps you should try saying them in the mirror."

"What do you mean?"

"Our hallways don't boast marble floors or Corinthian columns, but the lives you're affecting here mean as much, if not more, than your university students. Every awkward hug you give. Every procedure you streamline." He laughed. "Every car line you straighten. It also has deep down value."

They stared in silent communion. Two people who'd been disappointed in their dreams. Pushing each other to find the courage to dream again.

Something in a hidden space at the back of Victoria's heart loosened. It unfurled like a flower, took a deep breath, and released a sigh.

Perhaps her time in Sweetheart wasn't an accident. Wasn't a waste of time. Wasn't ... Did she dare to consider it? Wasn't temporary.

"Hey, people!" Micah's father burst through the gym doors and waved a thumb at the exit. "Check it out. This one's a doozy."

Victoria's stomach snapped into a tight knot. It couldn't be. Surely the vandal wouldn't have the nerve to paint while there was a crowd of people in the building.

Andrew and she hurried outside, where a group formed around the old, familiar wall. Phones were out and videos recording. Victoria pushed her way to the front.

A giant, haphazard crow's head, its black feathers sprayed in sloppy abandon, stared back at her. The painter must have worked at breakneck speed while everyone was in the gym. The expected speech bubble was there. This time, it wasn't a phrase she'd said herself.

Victoria read it without expression. "'Counting down until the end of the year. Goodbye, Ms. Bark!'"

Cameras turned her way. People waited for her reaction. Andrew placed a hand to her elbow in a protective gesture.

Victoria smiled. Knowing she had constant backup made life easier. Sweeter.

She walked to the graffiti and addressed the onlookers. "Ladies and gentleman, I have a feeling this will be the last unsavory picture you'll witness on our school's wall. Expect to hear more details soon. Thank you for attending the program, and have a wonderful night."

Chapter Thirty-Four

Victoria entered the gymnasium. The staff sat in one long row of metal chairs the custodian left in front of the stage. They talked while waiting for her to begin. Some laughed, but not all. From their disgruntled expressions, she suspected quite a few were grumbling about the emergency staff meeting she'd called after the program.

She whispered a silent prayer for wisdom. If this didn't work, there were no other leads to follow. She clapped. "Attention please."

The employees quieted.

"This isn't our ordinary time for a staff meeting, and I'm cutting into your weekend. Thank you for agreeing to stay."

"Did we have a choice?" someone called from the end of the row.

She gave a soft laugh. "Perhaps not. I appreciate it anyway." She raised her arm and tapped her watch. "I've set an alarm for ten minutes. I promise not to keep you any longer. But I'm hoping you'll be interested in these purchases I made."

Victoria walked to her purse and pulled out several squeezed-out tubes. She passed them to various people in the room. "You might not believe this, but I spent a bit of my youth clubbing in New York."

"You?" Mr. Beazley scoffed.

She laughed again. "Yes, me."

Andrew grinned. "I knew you must have learned those wedding dance moves somewhere."

Victoria ignored him and held up a tube. "This body paint was popular back then. You could apply it at home and ride the subway to the club with no one looking twice. But once you got under the black lights—"

She took a small flashlight from her bag, held it under her chin, and switched it on. Her audience gasped. The remnants of the mischievous college girl left inside of her giggled. She'd spent a brief five minutes in the bathroom painting the feathery mask. The small, handheld black light revealed purple and black feathers swirled around the upper half of her face in direct defiance to the unflattering graffiti that ended their program on a sour note.

"How pretty," Ms. Amy said. "My kids would love it. I should use it in the classroom."

Victoria chucked the sweet young woman on the shoulder. "Leave it to you to turn this idea into a lesson plan."

"Wasn't that why you showed it to us?"

"Not exactly."

Every pair of eyes in the room pointed her way. Waiting. Wondering what she'd say next.

"We've been unable to identify the person vandalizing the school. Even installing a secret camera didn't work. The footage told us the perpetrator's height. Not much else."

If she was wrong about this, any progress she'd made with the staff would be obliterated. They'd accuse her of targeting them. How could Victoria put her suspicions into words without driving them away?

"Show them your heart."

Her brother's advice rang in her mind. It went against her very nature. She prided herself on being self-sufficient. In control. Unshakeable. But if she wanted to win their hard-earned trust, she would have to be vulnerable.

Victoria discarded the paint tube on an empty chair. "I'll be honest with you. The graffiti freaks me out. I tried to pretend it didn't matter, but the whole thing hits me on many different levels. The organizer in me despises the chaos it causes among the students and parents. The control freak hates that I can't make it stop. And—"

She really didn't want to be this vulnerable.

Victoria glanced at Andrew. He graced her with a soft smile and lifted his chin, as if to say, *Go on. You're doing great.*

Her tutor approved. She must be on the right track.

She drew a breath. "And although I try not to take it personally, the ugly words prick my heart. I concede my methods have been uncomfortable for everyone."

A few nervous laughs echoed in the room.

"But I did what I thought was best for the school, for the children, and for you. If I was wrong—" She gulped. Her pride didn't taste so good going down. "If I was wrong, I'm sorry. And I—"

Looking around the room, Victoria had to acknowledge this was the most successful staff meeting of her elementary principal career. Each person focused on her, not a whisper or a wandering eye glancing at a cell phone.

"I need your help. I can't do this on my own."

"Can't do what on your own?" Ms. Amy blinked.

"I can't make Sweetheart Elementary everything it should be without you. Please trust my methods. Starting with identifying the person who's been defacing school property."

"You mean the graffiti?" Ronnie's eyebrows crinkled.

"Precisely." Victoria moved to the wall and placed her hand on the light switch. "I'm hoping my gut instinct is wrong, but I doubt it."

She flipped the switch, and the gymnasium plunged into darkness. The curtains were drawn tight over the high windows near the ceiling. She'd made sure the thick, metal doors at the entrance were closed and moved the chairs closer to the stage. Long black lights beamed from the floor.

Mr. Beazley's white dress shirt glowed. Pairs of teeth shone through the inky blackness as nervous titters sounded. A few phone flashlights popped up and waved around.

"Please," Victoria called, "turn those off. This is important."

They put the phones away. The darkness returned. She studied the shadowy forms as she walked around the group.

"Whoever painted the graffiti always uses the same spot. When I realized the vandal is someone from our school, I tried to provoke them with posters, expecting the culprit would show soon. And they did."

She walked to the light switch and flipped it on. "I truly hoped to be wrong, but these past two minutes confirmed my suspicions."

"You lost me, sugar." Ronnie scratched the back of her head. "Just what did you find out in the dark?"

Victoria paused. Should she reveal it to the group or confront the guilty party alone? She knew what the old Victoria would have done. Let the perpetrator suffer the consequences without consideration for their feelings.

She made a surprisingly quick decision. "I spread this paint on the wall last night and also before the program, hoping some might stick to the vandal's hands if they created new graffiti. When I turned off the lights, I was seeing if any of your fingers glowed."

Teachers' heads jerked as they eyed their coworkers.

Andrew's brow knit. Did he understand her methods or think she was carrying this too far?

"Who is it?" the PE teacher called.

She folded her hands. "I prefer to discuss this with the person one on one. Although it was illegal for them to deface school property, I don't plan to call the police. We don't want the children to hear how one of their teachers broke the law."

"You mean, you're going to let them get away with it?" Ronnie squeaked.

"Hardly," Victoria scoffed. "Sweetheart may have softened me, but I'm not that beneficent. No. I'm asking the guilty party to come and talk to me privately. We'll discuss an appropriate punishment that doesn't involve public censure."

Victoria scanned the room, her eyes meeting with the vandal's for the briefest of moments. "See you next week."

Chapter Thirty-Five

Belinda Carlyle sat on a chair in front of Victoria's desk, looking anywhere but at her. Teachers had entered the principal's office all day to discuss the upcoming testing schedule. No one would suspect their meeting was for any other reason.

Victoria clasped her hands on top of the desk and waited for the art teacher to talk first.

Belinda had delayed until most people were outside for the end-of-day dismissal. She tugged at the collar of her tie-dyed cotton blouse and tucked its hem tighter in her gauzy, floor-length skirt. The woman made eye contact and squirmed under Victoria's steady gaze.

Belinda drew a shuddery breath. "How did you figure out it was me?"

"The words alerted me it was a staff member. I suspected *you* because of the quality." Victoria hated to admit it. "The graffiti wasn't random splashes thrown from a paint can. I realized someone created the work with quick, precise details. That takes talent."

Belinda's shoulders hunched. "What do you plan to do about it?"

Victoria said nothing, and Belinda rushed on.

"Okay. I confess, it was a stupid mistake. A prank. People got a good laugh out of it, right?" She twisted the fabric of her skirt. "Besides, I doubt a little glow-in-the-dark paint on my hands would hold up as evidence in court. It's not like there was any permanent damage or anyone getting hurt or …"

Victoria bided her time until Belinda's words trickled off into tense silence. Then she spoke. "As I stated before, I don't plan to press charges. But you did something wrong and must make restitution."

"Re-sti-tu-tion?" Belinda waggled her head with each syllable. "What do you want me to do, pay the cleaning bill?"

"For starters." Victoria unfolded her hands. "I've gone back and forth in my mind over whether or not to fire you."

"Fire me?" Belinda jolted.

"One of a teacher's greatest responsibilities is to set a good example for the children. What if they found out you did this?"

Her lips drooped. "I didn't mean for them to ever know. I was just so stinkin' mad at you. Coming in here with your highfalutin outfits." She picked at a thread on the seam of her shirt. "Throwing everyone in a tailspin with your orders. Making life difficult. And …"

"And?" Victoria urged.

Belinda's defiant eyes jerked up. "And I hated how Andrew treated you. Different. Special."

Why did love have to be complicated? Helping some and hurting others.

Victoria stood. "I appreciate your taking the initiative and seeking me out. It would have gone harder if you didn't confess."

Belinda cowered in her seat. "Wh-what do you plan to do to me?"

"I'll calculate the bill for the hours spent and materials needed for cleaning. Once the wall has been fully restored, it will be your job to replace the graffiti with a more inspiring message."

"Huh?" Her cheeks rose as she squinted.

"You're correct that the students and parents enjoyed seeing the pictures you painted. You've shown your artistic talent in a negative way. How about we turn it into something positive? I'm commissioning you to paint a heart mural incorporating the names of all the children in the school with the words *We love them like they're our own.*"

"You mean, you're not going to fire me?" She sat straighter.

"No." Victoria strode to the door. "But please consider this a probationary period. If you do anything—anything—to cause trouble at Sweetheart Elementary, I will be terminating your contract without further notice."

Belinda sprang from her chair and hurried to the exit. "I—I understand. Thank you ... Principal Park."

Victoria nodded and opened the door. The art teacher stumbled out, and Victoria shut it behind her. Rolling her shoulders, she returned to the desk.

Someone knocked, and she sighed.

Please, God. Don't let that be a new problem.

"Come in."

Andrew entered. His sunny grin energized her like a triple shot espresso. She found herself smiling back.

"Hey." He stayed at the entrance, one hand on the frame. "I saw your car in the driveway when I left this morning."

"The wretched thing wouldn't start again."

"You could have ridden with me. How did you get to work?"

"My brother drove. It was early, and I didn't want to wake you."

"My offer to carpool stands." His eyes took on a naughty twinkle. "I admit, I may have ulterior motives."

Victoria bit back a laugh. She stood and walked to meet him at the door. "Thanks for the salacious offer, but you can't play chauffeur forever. I need a permanent mode of transportation. Even if everything in Sweetheart is within a ten-minute drive."

His smile faded, and his gaze traveled over her face. "You act like you're planning on staying awhile."

She paused. It certainly sounded that way. The words had spilled from her mouth without reflection.

Victoria fiddled with the bottom button on her jacket. "The idea isn't as reprehensible as it used to. But I don't, I haven't" —she looked down and scuffed her shoe on the carpet—"it's something I'll have to think about."

She dared a glance up.

His smile was back and growing by the second.

"Being open to new ideas." He nodded. "I approve."

"Aren't you supposed to be at dismissal?" She gave him a playful push.

Andrew caught her hand tight. "Just about to leave. Please allow me to say I applaud the new direction your thoughts are taking. Let me give you one more thing to think about."

He stole a quick kiss and then shut the door in a swift motion.

Victoria stood with feet frozen, her fingers reaching to touch her lips. A romance with a coworker was always a bad idea. Unprofessional. Unpredictable.

Yet she found herself humming as her cell buzzed. She sat, picked up the phone, and checked her messages.

Her hand stilled as she spotted a familiar name. Abe Wilson. Her friend on the university's board.

She clicked the message. Two words. *Call me.*

No details, just a directive. Short and sweet. Classic Abe.

Victoria checked the time. Three o'clock. It was an hour later in New York, and Abe usually left his office by four. Would he be at work?

She drummed her fingers on the desk. Waiting until tomorrow meant a night of tossing and turning. It wasn't like she worked for Abe anymore. What did it matter if she called him after hours?

She dialed his number and held the phone to her ear.

He answered on the first ring. "Victoria!"

"Hi, Abe. What did you need?"

The conversation took less than a minute. She hung up, slumped in her chair, and flopped her head to look at the ceiling.

"Really, God?" She glared at the water-stained tiles as if they held the answer. "Why now?"

ANDREW SNEAKED A PEEK AT VICTORIA ON THE PASSENGER SEAT. SHE quietly sipped the espresso he'd bought her at Heavenly Roasters after leaving the school. One of the *Brandenburg Concertos* played through the speakers, and he hummed along.

He could get used to this.

Her mind elsewhere, Victoria remained silent.

"Everything okay?" he asked.

She started. "What? Yes. Why?"

"You appear—what's the right word?—distracted."

She took another sip of coffee. "I suppose I am."

"Would this have anything to do with a certain art teacher's luminescent fingers?"

"You knew?" Victoria stared with eyes wide.

"Not until your black light trick. Belinda was sitting next to me. The tips of her nails glowed when the lights went out."

"Ahhhh." She placed her coffee in the cup holder. "Why didn't you say anything?"

"You're the principal." He shrugged. "I figured you'd handle it."

"Since when? You're always ready to jump in and advise me how to deal with the staff and students."

He drove onto their street and took a left into the driveway. Killing the engine, he turned. "Not this time. It's serious business. I know you'll make a fair but just decision."

The corners of her mouth curved the tiniest bit. "Have I ever told you you're my favorite teacher?"

His heart slammed to a halt in his chest and then raced forward like someone stepped on the gas pedal. Andrew pressed his lips together. He must be cool. He couldn't lift his arms and bounce on the seat like one of his students, no matter how badly he wanted to.

"Not surprising." He popped the door handle and climbed out. Ducking his head back in the car, he winked. "I'm everyone's favorite teacher."

She rolled her eyes.

He shut the door and trotted around the front. Victoria sat, concentrating on her phone, when he opened the passenger's side door.

Andrew tapped the car's roof. "I have a favor to ask."

"Yes?" Victoria slapped the phone face down on her lap.

He took a fortifying breath and extended his hand. "Are you up for going public?"

Chapter Thirty-Six

Victoria's fingers tightened on her phone, where a new text from Abe remained unread. She hadn't had time before Andrew opened the car door. Hiding it was instinctive. She felt like a student getting caught looking at a crib sheet.

"Public?" Her voice squeaked out. "What do you mean?"

Was he talking about their relationship? They weren't official yet. Wait. What did she mean by *yet*? They were never going to be official.

Not now.

Andrew rested his arms on top of the door. "Can you bring your violin to work tomorrow?"

She cocked her head. "Yes. Did you want to show the kids?"

"Sort of. I'm bringing my cello and thought we could play the Pachelbel duet for them."

Victoria put down her cell, slipped from the seat, and faced him. As he leaned on the door, it made their heights almost equal. She touched his arm. "You're going to play for them? Are you sure about this?"

He blew a dramatic puff of air. "No. But you were right

when you said it was okay to dream again. I need to get to work on a new vision. I'd love to raise future musicians as well as singers. This is a chance to provide inspiration. Maybe a student will hear me play"—he laid a hand on top of hers—"hear *us* play and choose the musician's path. They might even end up on the first chair that always eluded me."

Victoria's heart swelled in her chest. It oozed through her body and shot to her fingertips. She threw her arms around him and gave the tightest hug possible with a car door between them. "I know this decision wasn't easy. Good job."

"Hey!" He moved his head back. "Isn't that what we always tell the kids?"

"But it's true." Her oozy heart welled into her tear ducts. She blinked a rapid beat and attempted to stem the watery tide with a joke. "Pastor Thibodeaux might draft you for the worship team when he hears about this."

"Aw shucks." He snapped his fingers. "I guess it won't be so bad if you get drafted as well. Two instruments are better than one."

Her eyes cut to her phone lying on the front seat. She turned her back to Andrew and grabbed it, slipped the cell into her purse, and closed the car door.

"When do you want me to bring my violin to the music room?"

"Let's start with Sophie's class. They come first tomorrow morning."

She nodded in agreement, making sure to keep her expression neutral. A black fog of guilt replaced her elation. But she couldn't tell him. Not yet.

Better not to ruin this sweet moment with painful facts.

Chapter Thirty-Seven

Rich, beautiful sounds poured from their instruments as Andrew and Victoria played the Pachelbel duet. The climax of the piece approached, and their bows moved in tandem. The kids sat on their primary-colored carpet squares, eyes round, jaws drooping.

A movement by the door caught Andrew's eye. Several employees' faces crowded at the window, their eyes as wide as the students'. He couldn't blame them. Victoria was a sight to behold as she lost herself in the music. Her loose, black hair swished as her body swung. Passion sang from the strings.

They hit the last, glorious note, and the kids erupted. Clapping. Cheers. And one screamer he corrected with a disapproving glance.

After the class left, Victoria placed her violin in the case. She attached the bow to the clips at the top. "The secret's out now. All of Sweetheart will soon realize how their beloved music teacher is also a world-class cellist."

"I'd hardly say *world-class*." His shoulders may have broadened with her praise.

Her lips twitched. "Do you think Pastor Thibodeaux will

call before lunch or after with an invitation to join the worship team?"

Andrew moaned. "If he does, I'm going to throw you under the bus and suggest he take both of us."

Her smile faltered. She turned away, closed the lid of her violin case, and yanked the zipper shut with sharp, impatient motions.

"Hey"—he stepped in front of her—"I was joking. I wouldn't force you to play anywhere."

Victoria brushed the soft, padded top of the case. "The thought of joining the team doesn't bother me. I love every chance I get to play with you."

Her words were sweet, but she avoided his gaze. There was something more to this story. Something unpleasant. He might be inviting trouble but had to ask.

"Then why does your face look like I suggested you join a lawn-mowing team?"

"I expect I won't be around much longer to join anything in Sweetheart."

He scoffed. "Is that it? Why are you always pointing out your possible departure? You even considered investing in a new car. Who knows? Give it a few months. By the time the end of the school year rolls around, you may decide you've grown attached to Sweetheart."

Victoria moved away. She walked to his desk, sat on the top, and studied him with a serious expression.

He raised his brows. Was she going to give another speech about how her real life was in the big city? She might fight it, but Sweetheart was growing on her. He could tell.

Victoria sighed. "Yesterday, I received a text from someone at the university I used to work for in New York. The man the board elected as associate dean instead of me has made a hash of everything. He's come in late, misplaced important documents, offended a prospective donor, and gotten caught dating a student."

Andrew shook his head. "And they could have had you. Poor saps. Their loss is Sweetheart's gain."

She curled her bottom lip and bit it. "That's why Abe contacted me. He has enough board members convinced they made a mistake. They're ready to fire this new guy and offer me the position."

His body stilled. The quiet hum of his computer filled the room. In the corridor, a childish voice shouted down the hall.

Victoria stood straight and paced to the door. "I told Abe if the board approves me, I'll return to New York by next week."

"Whoa! Next week?" He moved forward. Catching her by the arm, he bent and looked her in the eye. "You're leaving now? Before the school year finishes?"

A burgundy head popped up on the other side of the door's window. The two of them jerked back. Mrs. Biddle's wide eyes took them in. Her heavily lipsticked mouth rounded.

Her muted voice carried through the door. "Victoria, dear! Are you going away so soon?"

Andrew almost slapped the glass. Did this woman have built-in radar? He flipped the deadbolt and led Victoria to the corner that couldn't be seen from the doorway.

He crossed his arms. "As much as I hate agreeing with Mrs. Biddle, isn't this a bit soon? What will the school do when you're gone?"

She lifted her chin. "I'm just a substitute principal. They'll find someone else. This position was always temporary."

"But what about the kids? What about Sophie? What about—"

His jaw locked. What else was there to say? He refused to descend to the pathetic level where he asked if she was leaving him too.

Wasn't it obvious?

No matter how much she'd opened up, no matter how many hearts she'd won over, no matter how comfortable she'd started to feel in Sweetheart, Victoria would always choose New York over them. Over him.

Once again, he'd come in second.

Chapter Thirty-Eight

"You're leaving?" Katherine vaulted from the couch. "You can't!"

Victoria squirmed on the gray armchair. Her sister-in-law and she had grown close throughout the graffiti stakeout but not close enough to shout at each other. There was still some level of courtesy expected between them. Although, Katherine didn't seem to think so.

Ryan caught his wife and tried to urge her back down. "Honey, stay calm. Let's hear Vic out first. Then you can rail at her."

Victoria gave him a dirty look. "Thanks a lot, Bro."

Katherine flopped on the cushions.

"Careful!" Ryan placed a hand on her arm.

She shooed him away. "This messes up everything, Vic. I was talking with Mattie Kilgallen yesterday. She's loving the stay-at-home mom role and doesn't want to give it up. I planned to ask the school board to offer you the position permanently. Are you sure you won't stay?"

Victoria smoothed the lapel of her jacket. "I never wanted to be an elementary school principal. You know that."

Ryan observed her with a critical eye. "But you were starting to adjust. Even enjoying it a little."

She shrugged. "It's not as bad as I imagined, but working in a university has always been the plan."

"Whose plan?" Katherine smacked the couch. "Yours? Did you bother to ask God what He thinks about this?"

Victoria's lips tightened. Her jaw jutted out.

Katherine nodded. "I'll take that as a *no*. Look, Vic. If anyone understands the pain of blindly rushing into things, it's me. You should pray before making such an important decision."

"Fine." Victoria managed a serene smile. "I'll pray about it. Happy?"

Ryan's cocked eyebrow communicated how much he doubted her sincerity. "What about Andrew?"

Victoria lowered her gaze and picked at the piping on the chair. "I told him today at school. He took it very well."

Too well. After his initial outburst, he'd accepted her decision with a nod and polite congratulations. Not at all the kind of reaction she'd expected from someone who'd kissed the fire out of her veins and back again.

"He didn't try to stop you?" Katherine slumped. "I thought you two really had something going. That it was only a matter of time before you made it official. Our kids would grow up with their cousins. Close. Like brothers and sisters."

"Wow." Victoria raised her hands. "You don't have kids of your own, and you're already anticipating mine?"

Katherine gently rubbed her belly. "Actually ..."

Ryan put an arm around his wife. "This wasn't the way we planned to tell you, Vic. But, we've got good news. You're an aunt."

"What?" Victoria poked her head forward. "I'm an aunt?

You two have only been married a few months. How busy have you guys been to—"

The couple smirked with matching twinkles in their eyes.

She waved her hands. "Forget it. I don't want to know. Oh my. This is—this is amazing!" She met Katherine in the middle of the room and hugged her. "I'm so happy for you both. But what are you going to do about being mayor?"

"Don't be ridiculous." Katherine swatted her. "I don't need to resign to be a mother. There's a daycare right across the street from the city hall."

Victoria laughed. She adored this crazy sister-in-law.

Ryan approached and wrapped his long arms around them both. "It's a shame the baby's aunt won't be here to babysit."

"Oh, right." Katherine leaned back. "You're leaving. How can you abandon us?"

Victoria drew her into another hug. "I'm sorry." She felt Ryan's warm fingers settle on the nape of her neck. "It's hard to leave. I admit it. But I have to follow my dream."

The Yorkies raced in from the kitchen and made laps around their family huddle. Ryan broke away from the group, picked up a dog with each hand, and gave his wife a kiss on the cheek. Katherine rested her head on his shoulder.

A mental picture flashed through Victoria's mind. It was the same pose but with Andrew and her as the loving couple. An ache started deep in her gut.

She shouldn't have eaten those red velvet sugar cookies Katherine offered her.

Victoria sat on her chair, then retrieved her phone from her purse. What day should she fly back to New York? Once away from all this happy-ever-aftering, she'd feel much happier herself.

Instead of like she was trading the fairy tale for the frog.

Chapter Thirty-Nine

Victoria pulled a cardboard box from the back seat and slammed the sedan's door. It caught at the wrong angle and bounced back. She dropped the box, lifted the door with both hands, and slammed it again. This time, it closed.

One more day, and she'd be back to taxis and subways. No more rickety, borrowed cars. No more hamlets with one stoplight. No more five-minute commutes to work.

The dark, misty sky lent an atmosphere of stealth to her early morning arrival at the school. Like she was sneaking out of town. But it was mere necessity. She had to pack up before the staff arrived.

And the questions.

Victoria pushed away the guilt. Leaving without a proper notice bothered her, but it couldn't be helped. Abe Wilson wanted her in New York on Monday to meet the board. If everything went well, and the current associate dean didn't gain a miraculous, last-minute reprieve thanks to his rich daddy, she'd be in her new office within a week.

An unexpected nostalgia hit as she walked toward the

building. She looked with fondness at the ex-graffiti wall and realized she wouldn't see the school spirit painting Belinda created. Would that plan get shelved after Victoria was gone?

She hoped not.

The playground. The bench where she'd sat with Sophie. The miserable iron grate where she'd broken a toe. Each one connected to a sweet memory.

Of hugs. And puppy stories. And being swept into a handsome man's arms.

Victoria had paid special care to keeping thoughts of Andrew in check. It was too easy to play the what-if game.

What if he was willing to move to New York?

Impossible. He'd rejected the big-city lifestyle. It would be wrong of her to take such a talented teacher away from Sweetheart. They needed him here.

But what if Andrew and she attempted a long-distance relationship?

Late-night calls. Seeing each other on holidays. Her making an extended visit in the summertime, when classes were out.

How depressing.

Victoria knew herself too well. Once she returned to the concrete jungle, she'd hop back on the hyperspeed hamster wheel of university life. As the associate dean, she'd be busier than ever. No time for romance or a personal life.

Or God.

Her head ducked as she entered the school, like the Almighty was holding a sign-in sheet and she was the tardy student. Sweetheart had shown her quite a few things she'd been missing. And the quiet peace that pervaded her soul and sent her attention upward was one of the biggest surprises.

She'd missed time with Heaven and leaning on Someone stronger than herself.

The last ten years of her life had been an endless circle of relying on her own strength and coming up short. Was she making the same mistake again?

Victoria shook her shoulders. Of course not! This second chance at the associate dean position was a blessing from above, an outright miracle. How could she refuse?

No sense devolving into a sentimental mess.

Victoria tapped her phone's screen as she passed the front counter and scrolled through her to-do list. Clean out her office. Turn the official paperwork over to Ronnie for whomever would take her place. Call a staff meeting for this afternoon to inform the teachers of her departure.

But this was Sweetheart. Half of them probably already knew. Who was she kidding? If Mrs. Biddle knew, everybody knew.

Victoria checked her list. Oh, right. Her violin. She'd left it in Andrew's classroom.

After making her way to his door, she paused. It was easier to retrieve when he wasn't there. If she kept herself busy enough, there would only be time for a brief, private goodbye before she left tomorrow afternoon.

She'd purchased the earliest plane ticket out of Dallas to forestall any painful speeches or drawn-out farewells.

Victoria sucked in a breath and entered the music room. Her violin case rested on a table. Andrew's large cello was propped against the wall at its side. He hadn't bothered to put it away. Unusual for someone who'd been a professional musician.

She approached the abandoned instrument and ran a hand across the smooth, polished wood. Her mind jumped to the night he'd played for her when she was sick. His musical pick-me-up beat any infusion from a hospital.

Victoria's lips trembled.

Oh no.

No tears from a big girl.

She never cried.

A renegade drop squeezed from her eye, calling her a liar. Followed by another. They chased one another down her cheek.

She collapsed against the wall and sank to the floor. Her head leaned on the curved top of the cello as if it were a friend's supportive shoulder. Covering her face with her hands, her breath broke in a sob.

Soul-deep wails poured from her mouth. Her ears rejected them. It must be someone else. Not her. Not self-sufficient Victoria Park.

Why did she have to be the strong one? Why couldn't she allow herself to be fragile for a change? Because right now, her heart was fracturing into tiny shards.

"God?" She raised weepy eyes to the ceiling. There was another water stain in the far corner by the wall. She should get the custodian to replace the tile.

Hysterical jags, a mix of laughter and tears, shook her. It wasn't her job anymore. Was it?

"God?" She tried again. "I don't want to."

ANDREW DRAGGED HIS FEET THROUGH THE FRONT DOORS BY A SHEER force of will. After Victoria ambushed him with the news of her departure, he'd tried to sleep, given up, and spent four hours aimlessly driving through the back roads with the windows down, railing at her and God and anyone else who happened to be listening at one o'clock in the morning.

What kind of Providence brought the perfect woman to Sweetheart, assigned her to the same school, allowed her to live next door, and then yanked her away?

When he'd calmed enough to stop the car at a scenic spot overlooking his favorite valley, realization hit. The person he was most angry with wasn't Victoria or God. It was himself.

He'd let her go without argument. Given up. Like a second-chair loser.

Not this time.

He hadn't bothered to go home and change clothes, choosing to stop at the school first.

Andrew braced himself as he walked to his classroom. He'd retrieve his cello and her violin, find Victoria, and give their relationship one more shot. Her car was already in the parking lot, so she must be here somewhere.

The idea of baring his heart terrified him. He was probably setting himself up for a monumental washout. But he had to try. To open his mouth and speak.

Or else he'd regret it every day until he was eighty.

An eerie moan echoed down the hallway, coming from the direction of his classroom. Had someone left a window up?

He hurried to the door, opened it, and scanned his room. His gaze landed on a pinstripe heap crumpled on the floor.

"Victoria!"

He rushed to her side and crouched. Her face was buried in her hands, her body heaving. Pitiful whimpers issued in fits and starts.

Andrew's fingers curled inward. Crying women were always a mystery. A crying Victoria was unprecedented. Even when she'd been fired, ridiculed in public, and broken a bone, she'd remained stalwart.

"Are you hurt?" His hands hovered above her shoulders. He wanted to touch her, soothe her, but the sight of her tears stymied him.

She replied with another shuddering sob, her hands still

over her face. It reminded him of when a kid skinned their knee on the playground.

"I'm sorry, sweetie." He rested his palm on the top of her head. "I can't understand you. Say it again."

Her hands lowered, and she lifted red, tortured eyes to meet his. "I"—she gasped—"I don't want to leave music."

He swallowed. Could she possibly be saying—

Andrew gathered her in his arms and tugged her close. "Please, Victoria." He rubbed a hand down her trembling back. "Please don't leave music. Or Sweetheart. Or me."

Chapter Forty

Victoria's first instinct was to lean away and stare at him. Make sure he was serious. But she remained in place and didn't interrupt.

Andrew's strong, steady fingers calmed the hysteric fountain of tears like a musician smoothing rosin on his bow.

"I love you." His voice resonated, warm and wonderful, against the ear she'd pressed to his body. "I love you so much, I'd consider leaving Sweetheart." His breath rattled. "I'm going to be honest. I don't know if I can do it. But for you, I'd try. I could apply for a position in New York. I'm sure there are schools there who need teachers."

Her lids slid shut. Angst and confusion evaporated. His offered sacrifice drove the final nail in the coffin. Time to bury ambition and trade her dreams of position and success for better ones. Dreams of home and family and a community where she saw the difference she made on a daily basis. And the biggest dream of all—Andrew. A man who matched all the jagged, hodgepodge pieces of her heart and pushed her to be better than she was.

And she would be better. With him.

Victoria whispered a silent prayer of thanks for the chance to dream again. God had forced her out of her comfort zone, straight into the arms of the love she didn't realize she wanted.

She pushed against Andrew's chest. Her eyes met his. She took his face in her hands and set a soft kiss on his lips. "You can't leave Sweetheart."

His brows dipped. The fear of rejection emanated in an almost tangible wave.

Victoria rushed to finish. "And neither can I." She smiled. "I can't leave Sweetheart or music or you."

He caressed the remaining tears on her cheeks with his thumbs. "You promise?"

She nodded. "I'll even seal it. But not right now." She scrambled to her feet. "Who knows when someone will walk by the window? Imagine the gossip if they caught the principal and the music teacher on the floor."

Andrew jumped up and pulled her back into his arms. "No one else but you would be here this early. At least give me one minute to kiss you properly."

"Okay. One minute. I'll set my alarm." Victoria couldn't tamp down her laughter.

Andrew's fervent gaze burned into her.

She wrapped him in an anything-but-polite hug that her after-school tutor would have been proud of and whispered, "I love you too."

Her words brushed his lips as his mouth descended and sealed hers with promises for the future and all the days and nights they wouldn't have to worry about Mrs. Biddle's head popping up at the window.

O*ne year later*

ANDREW WISHED RONNIE WOULD STOP ASKING HIM TO SHOW THE NEW parent volunteers around the school on his break. He needed a caffeine fix. If he hurried, there might be time to grab a cup of lukewarm coffee before his first class.

"What made you move to Sweetheart?" He escorted the woman down the hall.

"My husband and I decided it was time for a change. Raising kids in the big city is fine. But we wanted an old-fashioned way of life. More personal."

"You picked the right place. Keeping it personal is our specialty." He pointed a finger inside the cafeteria, where a group of children enjoyed their breakfast with noisy delight. "Some days, they might ask you to be an extra lunchroom monitor to make sure spaghetti doesn't end up on the ceiling."

She laughed, and he raised his eyebrows.

"I'm serious. Last week, we had two boys bet each other who could stick a noodle to the rafters."

The woman stared into the room with her neck craned as if she expected the pasta to be hanging like a party streamer.

Andrew waved a hand. "We already cleaned it off. Let's head to the front desk. Ronnie will give you an assignment."

They drew near the main entrance just as Victoria strode through one of the double doors. Her silky, black hair was smoothed into a serviceable ponytail. She wore a charcoal cable knit sweater and casual gray slacks with matching athletic shoes. In her hand, she carried a clipboard.

The mother leaned closer and whispered. "Isn't that the principal? I hear she's a tough cookie."

Victoria spotted them. "Mr. Zimmerman!"

"Uh-oh." Andrew's posture straightened. "I'm in trouble."

She swerved around a line of first graders, approached him, and held out the clipboard.

"You left this on the sidewalk at morning drop-off."

"I apologize." He took it from her. "Mrs. Gomez asked for an encore of my tardy sign-in song, and I added choreography to jazz it up."

"Choreography is fine." She stepped to the side to avoid the passing line of children. "But turn in your clipboard to Ronnie after the curtain call."

"Yes, ma'am." He inclined his head Victoria's direction. "Did you—"

"Good morning, Ms. Bark!" Micah launched himself at her from behind. "I'm the caboose today."

"Good morning, Micah." She rubbed his back in response. "But I've told you before. That's not my name. It's—"

"Oops. I forgot. Sorry." The boy laughed and raced to rejoin his line.

Victoria nodded at Andrew and his companion. "If you two

will excuse me, I have a parent conference in ten minutes. I'll see you later, Mr. Zimmerman."

"Looking forward to it, Mrs. Zimmerman." He winked.

Her expression remained impassive, but her eyes sparkled as she walked away.

He faced the new parent, whose mouth gaped wider than a goldfish's. "That's my wife." He pointed a thumb over his shoulder. "And you're right. She's definitely a tough cookie. But only the outside is hard. Once you get to know her, you'll find a soft, mushy center underneath."

"I heard that." Victoria's voice echoed down the hallway.

"Are you going to write me a demerit?" he called.

She spun and tiptoed back. "Are the kids gone?"

He checked both directions. "We're safe."

Victoria planted a quick smooch on his cheek. "It's been too long since you kissed me goodbye this morning." She wrapped an arm around his waist and addressed the parent. "Please forgive us. We're still newlyweds."

The woman beside him turned red as a preschooler throwing a tantrum. "I-I'm so sorry. I didn't mean to call you a-a—"

Victoria waved away the apology. "I'm used to making bad first impressions."

Andrew patted her shoulder. "But give her a few months, and you'll be a fan for life. She works harder and cares deeper about the kids than anyone in this school."

The woman smiled. "How did you two get together?"

Victoria and he groaned in tandem.

"Believe me," Andrew said. "It's an arduous story."

"We almost didn't make it." Victoria nudged him. "I had my plane ticket booked for New York City."

The parent observed their interlocked bodies. "What changed your mind?"

Andrew gazed at his bride. "We found out we make beautiful music together."

"The perfect duet." Victoria stared back.

"You know"—he flashed his brows—"if we added a couple little fiddles, we could play quartets."

Victoria's face pinched in her disapproving principal look. "Stop," she hissed. "It's not professional to talk about that in front of the parents."

He glanced to the side.

An empty spot remained where the woman had stood.

"No parents in sight." He grinned. "I guess she couldn't take the cringe factor. So, what were we talking about?"

"Quartets." His wife cocked an eyebrow. "I suggest we shelve this conversation until a later time. We can discuss it tonight. At home."

Andrew gave her a squeeze. "You promise?"

She granted him a quick peck on the lips before separating. "Sealed with a kiss."

He released a sigh of contentment. "I thank God every day for taking our shabby dreams and replacing them with something better."

"Way better." Victoria rose on tiptoe and enclosed him in a hug that surpassed any lesson he'd ever taught her.

-The End-

Acknowledgments

My students provide me with both fun and story fodder every day. Their creativity and unique perspectives open my eyes to the things I miss all around me. Scholars, thank you for being part of my life.

I also want to thank my Scribes critique partners who honed the early version of this story and the editors who polished the finished product and made it shine: Andrea, Regina, and Heidi.

Thank you to some of my own music teachers: Crystal, Melinda O'Donnell, Anne, and Joyce Scott. You played a role in this story. Thank you for being patient with all the times I didn't want to practice!

To Mom and Dad, you are the best part of my life. Thank you for raising me in God's house and always supporting the promises He gave me. I love you.

Shannon Sue Dunlap is a die-hard fan of happy endings and believes the Heavenly Father has designed one for each of us. She earned an M.A. in Journalism from Regent University, worked as a contributing writer for a Virginia paper, and wrote the novels *Lone Star Sweetheart* and *Love Overboard: A Novel*. Inspiration comes from everywhere—including her travels, her students, and the fun and flirty Korean dramas she enjoys watching. Even in the hard times, there's humor to be found. She tries to infuse every story she writes with moments that bring a good chuckle or an all-out belly laugh. One of her greatest hopes is that readers recognize themselves in her books since everyone is the hero or heroine in their own story.

Lone Star Sweetheart

Katherine Bruno's passionate, unfiltered temper makes her the
shrew of small-town Sweetheart, Texas. When she's drafted to help
the mayor's wife run against her own husband, Katherine meets
opposing big city political consultant Ryan Park. The good-looking,
flirtatious campaign manager gets under her skin, but fraternizing
with the enemy is off-limits.

Katherine must battle her lack of experience, campaign sabotage,
and her growing feelings for Ryan as she strives to succeed. His
unprejudiced acceptance of her strong-willed character beckons her
heart, but his jaded rejection of God is an insurmountable barrier.
Will Ryan return to his faith and stay with her in Sweetheart or leave
when the election ends?

Get your copy here:

https://scrivenings.link/lonestarsweetheart

Much Ado about Romance

A novella collection

The Marry Wives of Sweetheart by Shannon Sue Dunlap—Mrs. Augusta Page knows best—for her daughter, Anne, and the whole town of Sweetheart, Texas. When Anne's former boyfriend, Connor Fenton, returns after many years of absence, it's a rocky road to reconciliation. Connor attempts to rekindle their romance, but Anne's wounded heart never forgave him when he left her behind for the big city.

Augusta enlists the help of her longtime buddy Veronica "Ronnie" Ford to do a little matchmaking, but obstacles abound. Her husband is against the romance, and foolish friend-of-the-family John Falstaff has taken a shine to Anne and asked for assistance. But the biggest obstacle is her daughter's stubborn heart. Mrs. Page and Mrs. Ford have their work cut out to inspire Anne Page to join the ranks of the "marry" wives of Sweetheart.

The Tempest in the Bay by Susan Page Davis—A famous writer has retreated to an island home with only his daughter. For ten years, he's hidden away and not sent his publisher any new manuscripts. His daughter Violet is now 20 and wondering if it's time for her to see more of the world since her contact with the mainland is only through Darrell, a rather sluggish man from the shore community who brings out supplies once a month.

Paul's brother Barney and the CEO of his publisher's company set out on a yacht to track him down. But a storm intervenes, and when the sailing party lands on his island, Paul isn't sure he wants to go back.

Much Ado about Matrimony by Linda Fulkerson—Tricia Waters has resigned herself to the fact she'll never have a happily ever after, so she focuses on making her cousin's upcoming wedding a memorable one. But when she discovers her ex-fiancé is the best man, she vows to evade him. That is, until the two must work together to prevent the happy couple from breaking up.

Reeling from a personal tragedy, Dr. Ben McIntyre travels to serve as his buddy's best man only to discover the maid of honor is the love of his life. Or she was, until she ended their engagement six years earlier. He plans to keep his distance from Tricia. When circumstances keep pushing them to work together, Ben learns that avoidance is futile.

Get your copy here:

https://scrivenings.link/muchadoaboutromance

∼

Stay up-to-date on your favorite books and authors with our free e-newsletters.

ScriveningsPress.com